How easy, he wondered, would it be to walk the fine line between pretending to be Olivia's lover, and **wanting** *to be?*

And just where did that line begin and end? Because it was already blurred to hell and vanishing in his head. He figured he'd crossed it once already.

This is where the personal had to end, and the line be drawn strong and clear. And that is when he knew he would probably have to say goodbye to Olivia forever.

He could not allow his desire to be the downfall of the nation.

Available in October 2007 from Mills & Boon® Intrigue

Secret Alibi
by Lori L Harris

Diamonds Can Be Deadly
by Merline Lovelace

Dakota Meltdown
by Elle James

Rules of Re-Engagement
by Loreth Anne White

Automatic Proposal
by Kelsey Roberts

Haunted Echoes
by Cindy Dees

Look-Alike
by Rita Herron

Hell on Heels
by Carla Cassidy

Rules of Re-Engagement

LORETH ANNE WHITE

⊚™ MILLS & BOON®

Pure reading pleasure

*First published in Great Britain 2007
by Harlequin Mills & Boon Limited,
Eton House, 18-24 Paradise Road, Richmond, Surrey TW9 1SR*

© Loreth Beswetherick 2006

ISBN: 978 0 263 85756 6

46-1007

*Harlequin Mills & Boon policy is to use papers that are
natural, renewable and recyclable products and made from
wood grown in sustainable forests. The logging and
manufacturing processes conform to the legal environmental
regulations of the country of origin.*

*Printed and bound in Spain
by Litografia Rosés S.A., Barcelona*

LORETH ANNE WHITE

As a child in Africa, when asked what she wanted to be when she grew up, Loreth said a spy... or a psychologist, or maybe marine biologist, archaeologist or lawyer. Instead she fell in love, travelled the world and had a baby. When she looked up again she was back in Africa, writing and editing news and features for a large chain of community newspapers. But her childhood dreams never died. It took another decade, another baby and a move across continents before the lightbulb finally went on. She didn't *have* to grow up. She could be them all – the spy, the psychologist and all the rest – through her characters. She sat down to pen her first novel...and fell in love.

She currently lives with her husband, two daughters and their cats in a ski resort in the rugged Coast Mountains of British Columbia, where there is no shortage of inspiration for larger-than-life characters and adventure.

CAST OF CHARACTERS

Romeo – The military designation for the time zone in which New York falls.

FDS – The Force du Sable – a private military company based on the island of São Diogo off the west coast of Angola.

Biosafety level 4 – A level of safety from exposure to exotic, infectious agents that pose a high risk of life-threatening disease for which there is no vaccine or therapy.

The French Foreign Legion – An elite rapid-deployment force within the French military, established in 1831 and comprised of foreign volunteers, making it one of the most famous and legitimate mercenary forces in history.

The Republic of the Congo – A country west of the Democratic Republic of the Congo. Also referred to as Congo-Brazzaville.

The Cabal – A covert organisation that has been infiltrating the power structure of the United States over the past several decades and is now positioning itself to overthrow the government.

For more information, visit the Shadow Soldiers website at www.lorethannewhite.com.

Chapter 1

He stood across the street from United Nations headquarters, watching—a scarred man hidden in the shadows of bare-fingered trees. A wanted man. He didn't like being back on U.S. soil—illegally, no less. But he was here because he had to be. He was the only one who could stop an inordinately powerful man from bringing the entire nation to its knees in just six days.

And he needed a particular woman to help him do it.

She worked inside that building. She was the key to that man's inner sanctum, his Achilles' heel.

His daughter.

Jacques Sauvage thrust his hands deep into the pockets of his coat and narrowed his eyes into the brooding gray mist that was cloaking the city with premature darkness and chill. The trouble was, Olivia Killinger was also his *own* Achilles' heel. Her father had already destroyed him once because of it.

Six days—that's all he had to find out whether she was complicit in her father's scheme. If she was somehow oblivious to what Samuel Killinger was doing, he would have to turn her, force her to betray her own flesh and blood, the father she adored.

But if he found her guilty, he'd have no choice but to use her life as leverage against Killinger. Either way he could not afford to fail. If he did, millions upon millions of innocent people in the country's three largest cities—New York, Chicago and Los Angeles—would start dying by midnight, October 13. Just six days away.

And that would be only the beginning.

He hadn't seen Olivia in sixteen years. How in hell did one begin to bridge a gap like that? Especially when the woman you were waiting for had once been your fiancée—and you were supposed to be dead.

He checked his watch. She should have come out by now. The row of flags—almost two hundred of them— that had clapped bravely in the fall wind had long been wrestled to the ground by security staff, their poles now naked as the scraggy boughs above his head.

Only the blue-and-white UN flag with its olive branches of peace was left snapping against the front sweeping down from the Arctic, dragging the premature chill of the Canadian prairies behind it.

The irony of that lone UN flag flying in the face of

the coming storm wasn't lost on him. Global peace wouldn't stand a chance in hell if Samuel Killinger's plan succeeded. War would be his tool, the weapon that would feed his massive corporate coffers. Samuel Killinger and his Cabal were about to launch the U.S. into an era of violently aggressive imperialism that would kill democracy and forever change the shape of the globe's future.

Unless Jacques got to Olivia in time.

He checked his watch again. The temperature was dropping. Leaves skittered across the road, clattered and churned in the wake of a cab. It was fully dark now, the streetlights just fuzzy halos in mist. Still she didn't come.

He felt the first spits of rain against his face. Perhaps he'd missed her. Perhaps he hadn't recognized her profile among the huddled shapes that had scurried from the building into the streets, bent against the cold, making for home. Or perhaps she'd used a different gate. He shifted his feet against the growing numbness in his toes.

Then, suddenly, she was there.

Primal recognition slammed through him. His body snapped tight, and his nostrils flared, as if he'd somehow detected her scent on the chill wind. The muscles of his face grew taut, twisting at his scar as his world tunneled into just this moment. Just her.

The headlights of a car panned round and silhouetted her figure as she ran across the road, the wind playing with her coat like a malevolent spirit, opening it so that it fanned out behind her, pressing her skirt firmly against the outline of long, lean legs. She moved in his direction, her boot heels clicking on the pavement as she neared. His heart beat faster.

A sharp gust whipped hair over her face. She tried to hold it back with a leather-gloved hand, and he noticed she'd had it cut shorter. It looked more chic, but it was just as thick, just as lustrous. The sensation of his fingers combing through those soft waves of chestnut brown clawed through his memory. Jacques inhaled sharply.

Olivia Killinger could still do it to him.

One look was all it took to make him hard in places where memory had plagued him for well over a decade. But this time it was different. Now a ferocity swirled through the heat of his lust, and it fed a wild viciousness inside that scared him. Every molecule in his body screamed for him to storm into the road, grab her by the shoulders, yank her round, shake her, demand answers. *Why, Olivia? Why did you betray me?*

But he couldn't do that.

If he made one wrong step with her, if Samuel Killinger found out he was in town, the bombs would blow.

While he had to move fast, he also had to go in carefully. This operation was as delicate as it was time sensitive. And this was not supposed to be about the past, not now. This was about saving the future. This was about protecting democracy and innocent lives. To do it, he was going to have to walk a dangerous and delicate line.

Jacques drew in a steadying breath, and he took a step forward, the word *Olivia* forming in his mouth, a name that had lived indelibly in his brain for all these years but had never left his lips. Until now. Until this mission.

But as he stepped out of the shadows toward her, his hand rising involuntarily as if to reach out and close the distance of the years between them, a black SUV veered sharply out from the curb and screeched to a stop in front of her. She jerked to a stop. Her head whipped back, as if searching for escape.

Jacques instantly pressed back into shadow, the urge to rush forward and defend threatening to totally override his control. But he had to assess the scene. The vehicle was unmarked with an extra-long wheelbase and a battery of communications antennae mounted on top. When the door swung open, a man in a dark suit uncurled himself from the vehicle, stepped onto the curb, his eyes scanning the street as he moved. *Secret Service.*

Jacques swore softly to himself. This had just gotten a whole lot more complicated. What the hell should he have expected? The woman was dating the vice president. The woman who was once going to be *his* was now sleeping with the enemy—the very man Samuel Killinger was going to put into the most powerful office in the world in just six days. Acid filled Jacques's mouth as he watched.

The agent said something to her and gestured to the open door. She shook her head and stepped back from the car. The agent put his hand on her arm, his body language turning insistent. But she stood her ground, her posture defiant.

Intrigue whispered through Jacques. Why was she resisting?

The agent leaned closer, said something else to her. She hesitated and glanced in Jacques's direction. His heart stilled. Had she seen him? Could she sense him?

Then she turned back to the agent, and his heart dipped inexplicably. Of course she hadn't sensed him. Who was he to think she ever even thought of him? He no longer existed to her. He lived in the shadows. The damp chill from the nearby East River nosed into his coat. He flipped up his collar, watched her climb into the SUV.

He'd known she was seeing Vice President Grayson Forbes. He'd studied the tabloid photos of their outings. He'd been obsessed by one particular image where the vice president was touching her bare arm, their heads tilted together in intimate conversation. But Jacques hadn't quite anticipated how actually seeing the living evidence of her association would make him feel.

A cesspool of dark and conflicting emotions swirled up from somewhere deep inside him. He'd totally underestimated the depth of Olivia's hold over him, even after all these years. He'd misjudged the rawness of his latent passion, his buried anger, his violent resentment. He'd refused to acknowledge his deep and primal need for revenge. Until this very moment.

He knew in this instant, as the door of that SUV slammed shut, that this mission was going to challenge him in ways he hadn't even dreamed possible.

The SUV swerved out and pulled swiftly into the traffic. Jacques stepped into the street, raised his arm, hailed a cab, the wind snapping his wool coat around his calves.

"I'm with that black SUV up ahead," he told the driver as he climbed in. "Go where it goes."

"Follow that car?" The driver snorted. "Haven't heard that one in a while."

Jacques said nothing.

The SUV wove deftly, aggressively, through the evening traffic of the pulsing metropolis. His cab driver kept pace. The rain came down harder, flecking the windows, smearing light across the streets. Tires crackled over the wet surface, wipers clacked, and the traffic began to grow thick.

Then suddenly the congested stream came to a complete halt. Jacques wound down his window, tried to see what was going on. He could make out cops up ahead, stopping traffic. They allowed the SUV to pass, and hastily erected barricades behind it, barring all other access. Several police bikes with flashing lights and sirens swerved out of a side street, and joined the Secret Service vehicle in escort down the now-empty street. Jacques cursed.

Olivia had clearly been expected.

The traffic around them was now a stationary snarling mess, engines choking into the misty rain, dense cloud dropping even lower. His driver laid on the horn. So did everyone else, it seemed. Police were now trying to divert the bottleneck through narrow side streets. A chopper hovered somewhere in the cloud above, the sound bouncing heavily between buildings. The cab radio crackled, but the dispatcher's voice was drowned to Jacques's ears by the throb of the traffic and helo.

The cabby twisted his head over his shoulder. "Hey, buddy, you're out of luck. Dispatch says the entire block up ahead has been cordoned off—vice president has made an unscheduled stop in town." His eyes narrowed. "You *sure* you with that SUV?"

Jacques paid the driver and got out. He threaded his way through groups of reporters and photographers gathering along the barricades. A television news van honked as it mounted the curb, dispersing curious pedestrians. The rain was coming down even harder now, releasing the sharp smell of the city streets—a mix of gas, concrete and people layered over cool air. He'd forgotten the scent of New York. He didn't like it. He preferred the air of deserts and jungles, the feeling of open skies. He asked one of the photographers what was going on.

She told him the veep had slipped into town unannounced to the press, apparently for a private and impromptu dinner with an unnamed female guest. "Like we don't know who that is," she said, lifting her camera. "The entire street in front of La Bocca della Verita has been blocked off, and he's commandeered the hotel above the restaurant." She peered through her massive telephoto lens, focused. "Police are scrambling with the sudden security detail." She clicked. "Typical Forbes. Has to do everything with a high sense of drama. No wonder the president is running without this guy."

Jacques said nothing. He'd heard of La Bocca. It was a famous high-end Italian restaurant. He also knew Italian had always been Olivia's favorite. He stood against the barricade, stared down the empty wet street, his heart growing colder by the moment.

She glanced sideways at him. "Not a fan, are you?"

"No."

She smiled. "He does have fans. He's one of the most eligible bachelors in the free world." She pointed her camera at the phalanx of metropolitan police behind the barricade, readjusted the lens. "So much for privacy," she said as she clicked rapid-fire.

She repositioned her camera, trying to get a better angle down the empty street. "And so much for secrecy." She clicked, then glanced sideways at Jacques. "He's going to propose, I'm sure of it. Want to make a bet?"

"No, I don't." He reached into his coat pocket, found the slim, flat box, fingered the hard casing. He'd been uncomfortable with the idea of using what was in the box. He wasn't so uncomfortable now.

A bus came to a stop beside them in a cloud of diesel fumes, the side plastered with Vote Elliot posters. Jacques stared at the smiling image of the man who'd hired him— John Elliot, one of the most beloved presidents in the nation's recent history. There was no doubt in anyone's mind that he'd secure a second term in the upcoming election. But that was not going to happen if Killinger got his way before October 13.

There wouldn't be an election. Forbes would be president, and there would be no elections in the foreseeable future—the beginning of the end of democracy.

His job was to stop that from happening. That's why he was standing here tonight, in the cold streets of Manhattan, a city he thought he'd never set foot in again, preparing to face down a nemesis he'd never wanted to lay eyes on again, about to confront the woman he was once going to marry. A woman he thought he'd only ever touch again in his dreams.

He closed his fist tightly over the box. This was business. He could *not* allow it to become personal. The stakes were too high.

He turned his back on the photographer and the blocked-off street. If he tried to slip through those barricades now, he'd alert the cops and Secret Service. He couldn't risk that.

He'd wait at her apartment until she came home…*if* she came home, if she didn't sleep with Forbes in that hotel. She wasn't likely to bring the vice president back to her place. That would require some serious advance security planning, and it would generate the wrong kind of publicity.

Jacques crossed the street, dodging cars, oblivious to the angry honk of horns. Must be hell dating at that level. Not that he had any sympathy. Olivia was once going to be his wife.

Now she was positioned to become the First Lady of the United States. He cursed softly. He'd loved Olivia—mind, body and soul. He remembered how her skin felt beneath his. How soft the insides of her thighs, how…he jerked to a sudden stop, clenched his jaw in pain and lifted his face to the cold rain, his scar twisting tightly down the side of his face.

Her father must be damned pleased with himself. He'd gotten rid of that "poor bastard from the wrong side of the tracks." He was giving Olivia a president instead—a man of breeding, a man of wealth. A man befitting his little girl.

Rage mushroomed through his pain. He was going to look right into Samuel Killinger's eyes when he quashed *that* dream. He was going to show the megalomaniac bastard just what a guy from the "wrong side of the tracks" was made of. He was going to give Samuel Killinger a taste of *real* power.

Jacques swore bitterly as he reeled under the pressure of the emotions surging inside him.

He could see now there was no way in hell he was going to be able to keep the personal out of this. That genie escaped the bottle the instant he'd caught sight of Olivia again. This *was* personal. He was a fool for even trying to think otherwise. It was precisely because of his connection to Olivia and Killinger that he had been the unquestionable choice for this phase of the mission.

The best he could hope for now was to keep a tight leash on his feelings and to maintain his balance—and to remember, above all, that the success of the mission must come first. Above Olivia. Above him. Above this sudden ballooning need for revenge.

And in a few days it would all be over. He could get the hell out of New York and go back to the way things were.

He gritted his teeth and stalked with purpose into the city streets. He made for her apartment, his coat flying out behind him, images of her and Forbes searing his brain as the rain beat at his head.

Garish shades of neon—pink and yellow—slid over his features as he moved between the alleys. People in his path averted their eyes, stepped quickly out if his way as he approached, not because he carried a visible weapon. He didn't need to. His body was one, and he walked like he knew it.

He had a mission, and he was going to get it done.

* * *

The heavy wooden doors swung shut behind Olivia as she stepped into her favorite restaurant. The soft sounds of a harp and the gold light of hundreds of candles enveloped her instantly, but there was none of the usual buzz in the room tonight. La Bocca della Verita was empty of patrons.

Save one. And his entourage.

Vice President Grayson Forbes pushed back his chair and stood up from the only table set for dinner. "Olivia! I'm so glad you could make it." He stepped forward, arms held wide, an unusual animation dancing in his eyes.

An inexplicable sense of foreboding rippled through her. She glanced at the serving staff and bodyguards lined along the wall. "Grayson…what's this all about?"

"Surprised?"

She had a sudden, sickening feeling that things were about to come to a head, that Grayson was going to force her hand, and that she was going to have to tell him it was over between them. She'd been dreading this moment.

Grayson was not a man to accept rejection easily. He was like her father that way.

She'd planned on talking to him after the election, after he'd left office. She'd wanted to at least do him that courtesy.

"You…you're supposed to be in Washington," she said nervously. "What are you doing in New York? Why…why all this secrecy?"

He took her hands, drew her closer. "I wanted to have dinner with my girl tonight. No crime in that, is there?"

"Dinner?" She tried to smile. "You snarled up half of Manhattan and had me kidnapped by agents just for dinner?"

His eyes turned serious. He pulled out a chair. "Sit, Olivia, please."

She sat slowly, eyeing the bodyguards along the wall. "Do they really have to be in here?"

He didn't answer. He didn't need to. She and Grayson had been through this a hundred times before. He knew she was uncomfortable under their constant scrutiny. He'd learned just how much when he'd officially requested round-the-clock Secret Service detail for her, and she'd refused it, as was her right. After much argument, he'd relented. But when she was with him, it simply was not her choice.

Still, she didn't see why his men had to sit in on their private discussions—like now. It really wasn't necessary. It had begun to feed a growing suspicion in her that the exhibitionist in Grayson Forbes actually enjoyed the audience, the constant attention. It was just one more little reason that their relationship was beginning to wear her down.

He raised his hand, motioned to the sommelier. "I've taken the liberty of preordering your favorites, Olivia. Both wine and meal."

Even the music being played by the solo harpist was her favorite. Anxiety circled tighter. "Grayson, talk to me. What's going on?"

He paused for a moment. Then he placed his hands firmly over hers, looked into her eyes. "Okay, why wait? I want you to marry me, Olivia."

Shock slammed through her. She glanced around the room in panic.

A frown creased his brow. "Olivia?"

"Grayson…I—" She cleared her throat. "This…this is so sudden. I—"

He placed a finger over her lips. "Don't say anything. Not yet." He lifted her left hand and he slowly slid a ring over her finger.

Olivia stared at the shimmering cluster of diamonds set against cool platinum, and her mouth went bone dry. She could feel the staff watching from all sides. A buzz began in her head. She felt dizzy. Claustrophobic.

Her eyes flashed to his. "This is…so unexpected, Grayson." Why had she not seen this coming? Why had there not been a small sign, some warning that things had gone this far with him?

She liked him, always had. And she'd known him forever. His family had owned a holiday home near theirs in the Hamptons. Their parents were politically connected and they were friends.

Grayson was also devastatingly good to look at. He was rich, powerful, chivalrous, charming. And he made her laugh. He'd been obsessed with her since they were teens, but her heart had belonged exclusively to Jack.

And then Jack had gone and betrayed her—in love, and in death.

And even though he'd killed her cousin and fled from the law, he'd still managed to take a part of her with him—her soul.

He'd rendered her incapable of feeling again—*really* feeling. She'd gone through the motions, but not once had she ever come even close to experiencing the raw passion she'd known with him. Jack had made her come alive. When she'd been with him, she felt plugged in to the very rhythms of the universe, in tune with the resonance of life itself. It was absurd.

Maybe what she'd had with Jack was abnormal. Perhaps it was normal to be like this, sort of even and numb. But the fact that she'd tasted something exotic had ruined everything else. Because she knew it was possible. She knew it was out there—true love, raw passion.

But not with Grayson.

A sudden nausea swooped through her stomach. Guilt swamped her chest. Her hands felt clammy. "Grayson I…I'm sorry, I need some time. I need to think about this. We haven't—" she lowered her voice, conscious of staff "—we haven't even slept together in months. I thought that maybe—"

"That maybe I was losing interest?" He laughed easily, lightly, but she could see in his eyes that he was anything but taking this easily. He grasped her hands, a little too tightly. "Look, Olivia, no one said dating a vice president was easy. We have no privacy, no real time to ourselves, no policy book to follow. We're writing our own rules here. But we're *right* for each other. We always have been." He reached up, moved a lock of hair off her face and looped it gently behind her ear. "And that other thing—" he smiled "—I've arranged for a room tonight."

Panic kicked at her heart. She knew in this very instant how wrong this was. She could *not* sleep with him again. She'd allowed this to go too far. Her association with Grayson had been pleasant. He'd been good company during her deeply lonely times. He'd helped her see some of her major UN projects through the power halls of Washington. He'd given her causes audience before Congress and the Senate. With Grayson's alliance, she'd been able to help the less privileged people of the world—refugees, political prisoners held without cause, human rights abuse victims. Her work was her life and he'd smoothed roads for her.

She wasn't going to lie about it—Grayson Forbes had helped her help others. And that was partly why she'd kept on seeing him, partly why she'd slipped so easily into the convenience of the relationship, the friendship.

But she should not have allowed this to happen.

She honestly hadn't seen it coming. She'd been about to end it.

Olivia looked into his eyes, her heart twisting. She didn't want to hurt this man. And she didn't want to turn him down in front of all these people. It would humiliate him. It would make him furious. And fury in Grayson was a terrifying thing. He couldn't hide it as well as her father could.

"Grayson," she said firmly, "this is really bad timing for me."

His eyelids flickered sharply, and his fist curled over a napkin. She covered his hand gently with hers. "Please, give me a bit of time. I...I've been under incredible stress at work, with this refugee project, and the trial in the Hague. And—"

"You're making excuses, Olivia." There was a new

hardness in his voice, an edge born of hurt. "The timing is perfect. All those things you mentioned have just been wrapped up. I know this. That's why—"

"That's why I need a holiday, a break. Out of town. Just to get my thoughts together. I haven't been feeling myself lately."

His mouth flattened, and the light left his eyes. Her guilt deepened.

"Can we wait until after the election to talk about this?" she said softly. "When things have calmed down, when you leave office, maybe we can go away together, like normal people, away from the cameras, the press, the politics, bodyguards. We can talk about things." Her eyes pleaded with his. "Why now? Why the rush?"

"There is no rush. I've wanted this for a long time, Olivia. Much too long."

She took the ring off, her hands beginning to shake. She held it out to him. "It's beautiful. Everything is beautiful, the restaurant, the music. You. But I'm not ready."

He glared at the ring. Then he closed her hand so tightly around it she could feel the stones cut into her palm. His eyes burned into hers. "Keep it. Call it a thinking ring. Mull it over for a few days, and I'll give you another when you say yes." He smiled suddenly, falsely, reached for the bottle of wine, poured a glass for her and then himself. "Because I know you're not going to turn me down, Olivia."

She stared at the burgundy liquid still swirling in her glass. "I…I really think I should go, Grayson. I—"

"Come on, sweetheart, we've been together far too

long for games like that. You're here now, share a meal with me. Please." He raised his glass. "And let's have a drink—" His eyes narrowed slightly as he looked over the crystal rim. "To our future…and to your answer." He sipped, his eyes locked on hers.

Olivia reached for her glass and took a deep swallow—too deep.

22:58 Romeo. Olivia Killinger's apartment. Manhattan. Tuesday, October 7.

Jacques lifted the edge of the drape slightly with the backs of his fingers and watched the black SUV come to a stop down in the street outside her building. The agent opened the door, and Olivia climbed out.

His heart thudded quietly in the dark.

Another vehicle, some distance behind the SUV, pulled into a parking space behind a sedan that had been stationed across from her building since he arrived. Changing of the guards—there was more than one outfit watching Olivia tonight.

Whoever was in that sedan would have seen him enter her building. They would not, however, know that he'd been heading for her apartment.

He watched the way the row of yellow lights under the portico caught auburn glints in Olivia's hair. Then she disappeared. She'd be up any minute.

He dropped the drape, moved into position near the door, waited.

The elevator bell clanged softly down the hall. He timed it mentally, how long it would take her to walk down the hall. A key slotted into the lock, turned. His body tensed.

After sixteen years, he was going to hear her voice again.

Olivia paused. Something didn't feel right. It was as if there'd been a subtle shift in the chemistry of the air. She leaned toward her door, listened, but could hear nothing. She frowned, shrugged it off. It was her; it had to be. Her whole world had shifted on its axis tonight and she was just feeling off-kilter, that's all. She pushed the door open, stepped into her apartment and reached for the hall light switch—

A hand grabbed hers. She opened her mouth to scream, but another clamped down hard over her lips. She was twisted around sharply, dragged into the apartment. The door slammed shut—and all was dark. Panic punched her heart. She struggled maniacally, but the grip on her only tightened. Her attacker was male, huge and incredibly strong. His limbs felt like iron.

"It's all right, Livie," he whispered against her ear, "hold still, I'm not going to hurt you."

She froze. *Livie?* Only one person in this world had ever called her that, and he was dead.

"Relax." He spoke low, quietly, his breath warm against her neck. She could detect the scent of expensive aftershave. She could feel his coat was made of wool. "I'm not here to hurt you. I'm going to let you go. Promise me you won't scream, okay?"

The man had an accent. French—not Canadian French, continental French. Yet there was something familiar about the timbre of the voice, the way it curled through her, stirring something dark and forbidden in the depths of her soul. Her chest constricted like a vise over her lungs. She couldn't breathe. Her vision blurred.

"Did you hear me?" he whispered.

She nodded her head. He released her mouth cautiously, waiting to see if she would scream. She didn't. He turned her slowly round to face him, and he flicked the light on.

And her heart stopped.

Chapter 2

She looked up into his eyes—unmistakable eyes—ice gray and crystal clear. They sliced into her like a laser, flaying her open right down to her soul. No other eyes could do that to her. She'd never, ever seen eyes quite like his.

It was Jack.

Olivia tried to swallow, tried to get a grip on what she was seeing right here in her apartment—Jack Sauer. *Alive.*

But he was older, harder, colder—with a vicious scar that sliced down the left side of his face, along the sharp angle of his cheekbone, down to his mouth.

Curving his lips into a subtle, permanent—if sexy— sneer. It made him look dangerous.

It reminded her he was a felon, wanted by the FBI for the murder of her cousin Elizabeth. It reminded her he was supposed to be dead—killed by a grizzly in the Alaskan wilderness north of Mount McKinley.

And he was blocking her door—the only way out.

Her heart began to race. Fear whispered in the periphery of her mind. Her cell phone was in the purse that she'd just dropped to the floor. She was trapped.

Questions scrambled wildly over each other, tangling in her mind until she could hold no one thread straight. If he was alive, why had he not contacted her once in sixteen years? Why was he back *now?* Where had he been all this time?

"Jack…?"

"Jacques," he said. "It's Jacques Sauvage now. Jack Sauer died a long time ago, Olivia."

She stared at him. This was impossible. Moose hunters had discovered his wrecked camp in the trackless Alaskan wilderness. They'd alerted rangers who had found ID, his books, clothes, his shotgun, spent shells—evidence of a grizzly attack. DNA had proved the blood in the camp was his. Rangers had said it looked like he'd wounded the bear before being dragged off himself.

"God, it's good to see you again," he whispered darkly as he touched the small gold locket at her throat, his fingers brushing her skin.

A jolt of sexual recognition ripped through her body so sharp, so fierce, and so totally inappropriate, that she gasped, tried to jerk back. But he tightened his grip, held her close.

"You kept it," he said, lifting the pendant. "All this time, and you still wear it."

Her eyes began to water. It really was him. One touch and her body was alive, responding to his, whether her mind followed or not.

"Wh-where have you been?" Her voice came out in a hoarse whisper.

His eyes burned into her, devouring her, sucking in every little detail he'd missed over the years. She felt as if he was stripping her, slowly, layer by layer, down to the naked core. Her heart pounded, her breath became light, her vision narrowed. Hot and cold swirled with fear through her stomach and laced with an aliveness so sharp it scared her.

"Time has been good to you, Olivia," he said, his voice low, slow, his accent so seductively foreign. His eyes followed the curve of her breasts under her cashmere sweater. "Very good."

Olivia swallowed. This was a man accused of murder. She didn't know him anymore. She had no idea what he was capable of, what he'd become.

"Talk to me, Jack. Why are you back, what happened, where have you been all this time? What are you doing here in my apartment?"

He moved his hand from the pendant, stroked the curve of her neck, his skin rough against hers. Her knees went weak and her brain went completely blank.

He bent his head, his lips almost touching hers, his breath warm and soft as a feather. "I need your help," he whispered. "It's a matter of national security—" He sighed deeply. "Do you know how much I've missed you…how I've missed this…" He slowly pressed his lips over hers, covering her mouth completely. Heat melted her belly. Her breathing became ragged. She was incapable of pulling away.

He moved his lips gently over hers as he reached around her waist and slowly drew her body against his. He was giving her time to fight back, to jerk away. He was making this her decision as much as his. Yet she could feel his body shaking, his muscles straining to hold back the raging hunger that surged through him. He still wanted her, badly, and her body was burning in response to his.

The man she'd loved with all her heart was back in her arms. Holding her, kissing her, hard with need for her. Emotion imploded through Olivia. Tears burned her eyes, spilled freely down her cheeks, washing away the years. So many, many lonely nights, she'd dreamed that one day she'd feel his lips over hers, melt under his touch again. Suddenly nothing mattered but this moment.

Her thoughts spiraled into dizzying blackness as he increased the pressure on her mouth, filling her with his tongue, his movements growing rougher, harder, urgent, the salt of her tears mingling in their mouths as their tongues tangled and her heart twisted.

He tasted wild, foreign, dark—yet familiar. Her heart pounded. She leaned into him, opening to him, a raw hungry force driving her. She touched his face, guided him deeper, closer…and suddenly she felt the rigid line of his scar under her fingertips.

Reality exploded sharply through her brain. She stilled. She slowly traced the line along his cheekbone to the corner of his mouth. He felt the question in her touch.

"The bear," he said simply, covering her hand, drawing it away from his face and pulling her back to him.

The bear that was supposed to have killed him.

This time she resisted. "No…no, Jack. Please…. I…I don't know what just happened. I…I don't want this."

She forced herself to take a step back. He let her, his eyes watching her intently, arousal etched into his rugged features.

Her breaths were coming light and shallow. Her lips still burned. Her body was still hot, her hair a mess. She felt awkward, confused. And more than a little afraid— of him, of herself—of what had just happened.

"What…what do you mean, you need my help? And what about national security?" She nervously twisted the new ring on her finger as she spoke. "Does this have something to do with Grayson?"

His eyes followed her hands. When he saw what she was fiddling with, his expression changed instantly. A small muscle began to pulse at his jawline.

Olivia suddenly felt absurdly embarrassed to even be wearing the ostentatious cluster of diamonds. She had no intention of keeping it. The only reason she had it on right now was because she hadn't had the guts to hurt Grayson's feelings in front of all those people.

She covered the ring, pressed her hands against her stomach, trying to quell the tempest of emotions roiling inside her. Why should *he* be making her feel guilty?

He was the one who had betrayed her. *He* was the one who left her. *He* let her think he was dead all these years. Why should she feel even vaguely compelled to explain why she was wearing Grayson's ring?

He lifted her eyes to hers. "We have a lot to talk about, Olivia. May I come in?"

"You *are* in." In more ways than one.

"I need you to invite me, Livie."

She stared at him—powerful, deeply tanned, his dark hair cut aggressively short and shot through with the silver of time—and hurt filled her. In all these years he hadn't bothered to let her know he was alive. He had destroyed her when he'd fled, he'd left her to bleed. He'd stolen her youth. And now here he was, standing very much alive and healthy in her hallway. Anger whispered quietly around her pain. And she let it come. She needed answers.

"May I come in, Olivia?" he said again.

She held her hand out to her apartment. "Sure. Please, come in. Please come back from the dead, Jack. Please walk right back into my life, into my home." Tears threatened again. She blinked them angrily away. "Why don't you come right in and mess with my life all over again. It's not like you didn't get it right the first time."

Something hot and dangerous flashed in his eyes.

But the bitterness growing inside wouldn't allow her to stop.

"Would you like a drink, Jack? How about sitting on my sofa over there and telling me where you've been for sixteen long years, and why you've *really* come back to mess with me."

"A drink would be nice, thank you," he said, shrugging out of his coat. He walked right past her, into her apartment. He draped his massive black coat over her white chair and moved straight to the window. He lifted her curtain slightly with the back of his hand and peered down into the rain-drenched street.

She stared, dumbfounded. What on earth was he doing? She took in the expensive cut of his elegantly tailored black pants, his white silk shirt. He looked as if he'd walked straight off one of Europe's fashion runways. But while his clothes gave him an air of global sophistication, they did little to tame the wild ruggedness that literally pulsed from him. Who was this man? Who had Jack become?

She glanced at the phone on the wall.

"You're free to call whoever you like," he said without looking at her. "But I wouldn't advise it, not until you've heard me out."

She stared at him blankly. She should run. Now. Get out while she had access to the door. She should alert the police. Yet a desperate curiosity rooted her to the spot. He was once her lover, the man she'd was going to marry. And he was here, back in Manhattan, in her apartment. She *needed* to know why, where he'd been. She pushed her hair back from her face.

She could do this.

She could handle Jack Sauer. She'd handled way worse in international courts. And once she had her answers, she'd call whoever she needed.

She cleared her throat. "You still drink scotch?"

"Yes."

She retrieved the purse she'd dropped at the door, and moved over to the drinks cabinet, her heart thumping. She positioned her back to him as she slid her slim cell phone out of her purse and slipped it into her pocket. She wanted to be ready to call 911.

She removed the stopper from a decanter and began to pour whiskey into a crystal glass. That's when she realized how badly her hands were trembling. She closed her eyes for a moment, steadied her nerves. Then she poured a drink for him and one for herself. She needed it.

She picked up a glass in each hand, sucked in her breath and turned to face him. And her resolve crumpled instantly.

He was watching her so intently she almost forgot how to walk. She tried to force her legs to move smoothly across the wooden floor, tried not to trip over the white rug. She held a glass out to him. He took it, his fingers brushing slowly over hers as he did, his eyes never leaving hers. He lifted the rim to his lips, slowly sipped, eyes still locked with hers.

Something hot and foreign and dangerous slipped down into her stomach again. She put her own glass to her lips, took a gulp.

"Who's tailing you, Olivia?"

She choked on her sip. "What?" Her eyes watered as whiskey burned down the wrong way.

"Who's following you?"

"No one's following me."

"Take a look," he said, lifting the edge of the curtain for her. "See that silver sedan there, across the road?"

She edged forward, wary of touching him again, afraid of what would happen to her body again. She peered down into the street, conscious of his expensive scent, the quiet powerful energy vibrating from him. "Where?"

"Under that oak, right across from the park."

She saw it. "Don't be ridiculous. That car's not tailing me. *No one's* tailing me."

He remained silent, watching her, trying to read something. It made her nervous.

"It…it's probably someone looking for *you*. The FBI maybe."

He ignored the gibe. "That sedan came in right behind the Secret Service vehicle that dropped you off tonight, Olivia. After your dinner with Forbes." His eyes searched hers for reaction.

She looked sharply away. She didn't want to show him how her evening with Grayson had affected her.

"There was another vehicle waiting under that tree there, watching your apartment, before your SUV approached. It left as you arrived, and that silver sedan pulled in behind it, replaced the watch."

Something about his voice made her think he might be telling the truth. "It must be the Secret Service, then," she said, unsure now. "Grayson wanted to get security detail for me, but I told him I didn't want it. Maybe he got it anyway. He…he's not an easy man to turn down."

"I know."

The sudden dark edge in his voice shot a shiver down her spine.

"But that's no Secret Service detail out there, Olivia.

That's a private outfit—same bunch that was waiting for you outside the UN building."

"*You* were at the UN?"

"Saw you being whisked off for your private dinner with Forbes." His eyes drifted down to her ring.

How long had he been following her? Why?

"Jack, you're making me nervous. Please…tell me what in hell is going on? Otherwise, I…I'm going to have to ask you to leave."

"Did you get that tonight?" he said darkly, his eyes still fixed on her ring.

It was not his business. She didn't have to answer. "Yes," she said.

He lifted his eyes, met hers. "So he proposed, and you accepted."

No, I didn't. She wanted to say the words, scream them. But she couldn't.

"Do you love him, Olivia?" he whispered. "Do you really know this man? Do you love him like you used to love me?"

Emotion welled up so sharp and hot it hurt, filling her eyes, choking the words in her throat. She began to shake inside. "Damn you, Jack Sauer," she said quietly. "You left me, sixteen years ago, and you come back and ask me this, *tonight?*" Her voice caught. "It's not your business who I love. Not anymore."

The corner of his mouth, where it met the scar, twitched. "It's become my business, Olivia."

"It can *never* be your business. You have no right to ask who I love or choose to marry or when. You threw that right away, Jack, forever, when you killed Elizabeth."

His eyes narrowed. "Is that what you really think?"

"What else was I supposed to think?"

His jaw steeled. The muscles along his neck went hard.

Olivia took a step back. "Look, Jack, if you don't tell me what you want from me and why you're here, I'm going to call 911." She reached for the cell phone in her pocket as she spoke.

"I've come for your father, Olivia."

She froze. "I beg your pardon?"

No emotion showed in his face now. It was hard as steel, and his eyes had turned sharp and cold. "Those men outside, I think they're his. I'll have my guys check into it."

"*Your* guys? *What* guys? What are you talking about!"

He said nothing, just watched her eyes.

"Okay, you're making me really nervous. Leave now, or I'll call the cops."

He took a step toward her, and she lifted her cell phone. "I mean it, Jack—" She flipped it open, began to press.

Jack grasped her wrist and removed the phone from her hand. "Your father is involved in a plot to overthrow the U.S. government. But then, you might know that already, Olivia. I'm here to stop him, and you if need be."

"*What* did you say!"

He was still holding her hand, his fingers circling tightly around her wrist. Panic wedged into her throat. Her eyes shot to the door.

"Samuel Killinger and his Venturion Corporation board comprise a covert organization that refers to itself simply as the Cabal. This Cabal, under your father's leadership, plans to hand Grayson Forbes the most powerful office in the world." His eyes narrowed. "He plans to make your fiancé the leader of the 'free world' six days from now. That's all the time I have to stop them. That's what I've been hired to do. That's what I intend to do. And you *are* going to help me do it."

She tried to jerk free, but his grip tightened. He pulled her closer as he reached into his pocket with his other hand, took out a black box.

She yanked frantically against his hold. "Let me go, Jack! This is garbage! It's not possible. You…you're insane. And he's *not* my fiancé. I did *not* agree to marry him."

Something—hope?—flared hot and sharp in his eyes. Then it was gone. "That helps," he said darkly. "We have until midnight, October 13. If we fail, a set of biological bombs will be released over New York, Chicago and Los Angeles at one minute past midnight. Repercussions will be felt around the globe." He paused. "I hope you are not involved, Olivia." He snapped a metal cuff around her wrist.

Her brain reeled wildly. "What's this!"

"That's insurance, just in case you choose not to help me."

She stared in shock at the thick band of silver locked tight and cold around her wrist. It was the color of platinum. Smooth. Alien. And it had a strange little window cut into the top that held what looked like a glass ampoule of pale liquid. She looked up, terror filling her heart. "What…what's in it?"

"A GPS device. If you run, we'll know where to find you."

"Who's *we?* What's that *liquid* in the capsule?"

He studied her in cool silence, his eyes still seeking something in hers.

He was looking for guilt—that's what he was doing! Her heart began to palpitate. She couldn't breathe. "Tell me what the liquid is, Jack!"

"The capsule will break if you try to take the cuff off," he said flatly. "The liquid inside…it'll kill you, Olivia."

"What!"

He dropped her hand, stalked over to the drinks cabinet, poured another scotch, turned to face her. "It holds a lethal pathogen." He sucked back his drink, winced as it hit his gut.

"What *kind* of pathogen?"

"A very rare one. One that has been genetically modified in a lab run by the Cabal. Your father will know exactly what that pathogen can do. It's a variant of the one he plans to release in six days if President Elliot refuses to step down and hand power to Forbes by the October 13 deadline." His eyes lasered into hers from across the room. "I advise you to keep the bracelet on, Olivia. If you want to live, that is. You'll be safe as long as no one tries to cut it off."

She lurched toward him. "Take it off, Jack. Please. For God's sake, don't do this to me."

He shook his head. "I'm sorry, Olivia. I can't take it off."

"What do you mean!"

"You need specialized equipment to remove it. You need the antidote at hand…in case something goes wrong."

Blood drained from her head.

"You'll be fine, as long as you cooperate with me." He hesitated. "As long as I can trust you."

"I…I don't believe this is happening. What made you like this, Jack?" She held out her wrist. "You loved me once! How…how could you do this to me?"

"How could I hold one life against a billion others?" He gazed at her, hard, his eyes narrowing.

"One life versus world peace? What would *you* do, Olivia?"

23:59 Romeo. Manhattan.
Tuesday, October 7.

A green dot flared onto Grant McDonough's screen and began to pulse. *Bingo.* He flipped open his satellite phone, punched the number for the FDS base on São Diogo Island off the Coast of Angola. "He's in. GPS cuff has been activated."

"You have a detonator?"

"Affirmative. We both do. Antidote as well. Everything's in place."

"Good. Now we sit tight and wait for Sauvage's direction."

McDonough hesitated. "Any word on December?"

"He's been airlifted from Djibouti to the hospital here on São Diogo. His condition is critical, but stable. They still have him on life support."

McDonough flipped the phone shut, stared at the pulsing green dot. December had been shot in the gut by a mysterious pale-skinned man while helping evacuate Rafiq Zayed and Dr. Paige Sterling from the shores of Hamān. December sure as hell better pull through—for more reasons than one. They'd dubbed the shooter the Achromat because of his absence of pigment, and if he was found to be somehow affiliated with Killinger—McDonough shook his head. He didn't want to begin to think of what Sauvage might do to Killinger's daughter if December didn't make it.

He punched in a text message, letting Sauvage know that the vehicles outside Olivia Killinger's apartment had been traced to an outfit owned by one of the Venturion Corporation subsidiaries. It was a group that Samuel Killinger used for his personal protection and security detail. The maniac was having his own daughter tailed.

He pressed the button, sent the details.

Chapter 3

She stared at the silver cuff, her face sheet white.

Jacques hated this. His mouth felt like ash. His chest hurt.

"You said someone hired you to do this? Who?" Her voice was strangely flat.

"The president."

"President Elliot?"

He nodded.

She reached for the back of the sofa, steadied herself. "That's…ludicrous," she said quietly. "If…if the president really were threatened he'd go through regular channels—Homeland Security, the Secret Service, the military, CIA, FBI. Why on *earth* would he hire you?"

He studied her, searching for a sign, something that would betray her knowledge of this. He couldn't see it. Her reaction had been visceral, her shock too real. Unless she was damn good—unless she had learned from her father.

But he didn't think so. She was still wearing the small Saint Catherine's pendant, and that told him something.

He'd given it to her for her nineteenth birthday when they were both prelaw students. Saint Catherine was said to be the patron saint of lawyers, barristers, jurists, and according to legend, had been prepared to die for her belief in good. Jacques had never been as big on faith as Olivia's family, but the locket had been a symbol of what they both shared—a joint vision for justice, a dream of the future, a goal for their careers—a goal that had defied her father's insistence she become a corporate lawyer for one of his transnationals.

Instead she chose to work for the UN. And she still wore his pendant. It made a fierce kind of pride burn inside him.

And the fact she'd rejected Forbes fed him with a hot flare of hope that she was not so intimately involved with the vice president as to be a part of his scheme to take control of the White House. It also made a dark part of Jacques wonder if there might still be a place in her life for *him*.

He sipped his drink, welcoming the way it dulled the edge of his guilt, the pain this caused him.

"He can't use any of those organizations, Olivia.

The president's own Secret Service has been infiltrated. Elliot is being held hostage by the very system designed to protect him, his every move watched, every conversation recorded. If he so much as even *thinks* of engaging any agency traditionally at his disposal, those bombs *will* go off."

He paused, still watching her keenly. "Your father's corruption and connections go so deep that they root into the very foundations of the nation. This so-called Cabal of his has managed to infiltrate almost every level of government, commerce and the military over the past three decades. Elliot's *only* option was to try and secretly enlist an organization free of *all* U.S. overseeing or restriction, something outside the system. Way out."

"You?"

He nodded. "And if your father gets even a hint I am here, he will release those bombs instantly."

Olivia sank slowly down onto the white sofa. She leaned back, closed her eyes, her lashes dark on bloodless skin. She let her hands rest limp in her lap.

She was in shock.

She *had* to be clean.

But he could take no chances. Even if she knew nothing about what her father was doing, he must never underestimate the power of a blood bond. Especially under duress. It had destroyed him once before.

As much as he hated the idea, she'd have to wear the bracelet.

His satellite connection vibrated in his pocket. Jacques took it out, checked the text message from McDonough. So it *was* Killinger's men tailing her. He returned the phone to his pocket, wondering how she was going to take this news.

He'd already dealt her two severe emotional blows in a matter of minutes—coming back from the dead and accusing her father and Forbes of treason.

She was going to need time to process this. If he hit her with too much too soon, she could crumble or resist without thinking first. If she really was innocent, he wanted to get her to a point where it became *her* choice to turn in her father. He checked his watch. Unfortunately, time was a not a luxury he could afford.

She opened her eyes suddenly.

His heart quickened.

"Why should I believe you?"

"Because it's the truth."

She stared at him with a look so intense it drilled right to the very marrow of his bones. He met her gaze, held it. Her grandfather clock ticked loudly. He moistened his lips. A full minute passed.

"I want to know, Jack," she said suddenly. "Everything. I want to know who you're working for, where you've been. What happened all those years ago…on the beach…everything."

He nodded his head slowly, then seated himself on the sofa opposite her, the glass-topped coffee table between them. He leaned forward, resting his elbows on his knees, cradling his drink in both hands. He rolled the glass slowly between his palms, watched the liquid refract the light as it swirled around the faceted crystal for a few moments, then he looked up.

"When I left New York, I made my way through

Canada to Alaska," he said. "I thought I'd be okay, living alone in the wilderness, but it began to wear heavily on me. I didn't want to exist like that, alone and on the run. I wanted a life. I wanted to find some place I could hold my head up high." He stared into his whiskey, his mind going back where he seldom allowed it to tread. "Then I came across a copy of a newspaper, and I saw that my mother had died." He looked up slowly, met her eyes. "The paper was three weeks old."

Olivia leaned forward. "They said it was shock, Jack." She spoke softly. "They said her heart couldn't take the news of…of how you managed to flee just minutes before they came to arrest you."

His chest tightened. His scar pulled at his mouth. He inhaled deeply, killing his feelings. "I used the grizzly incident to disappear," he said, his voice studiously emotionless. "I got myself to the coast, got a fishing boat to take me across the Bering Strait to Russia. Made my way down to France from there. Joined the French Foreign Legion, fulfilled my contract, got a new identity and French citizenship in exchange."

She remained silent. He could practically see her heart beating under the soft white cashmere.

He sucked back another sharp swig of scotch, felt the comforting burn in his chest. He set his glass on the table, pushed it away, remembering how many nights he'd used the stuff to numb himself. How he'd done it again in that small Parisian bar sixteen years ago, the night before Jack Sauer disappeared forever, the gates of Fort de Nogent clanging shut behind him. No more memories. No more past. No more Olivia.

Until now.

He lifted his eyes slowly. "They call it the Legion of the Damned," he said.

"I know." She had a strange expression on her face, as if she was beginning to understand something about him. "It's one of the greatest mercenary armies of all time. One of the harshest." She paused. "I've read the literature, Jack. The Legion was created by King Louis Phillipe in the 1800s in the conquest of Algeria, and it's been a last resort for society's misfits ever since. It accepts refugees, revolutionaries, poets, princes, paupers, criminals—no questions asked."

"Not exactly—"

"You serve a minimum five-year contract. And *if* you survive, you have the option to be rectified—get a new name, usually the same initials, and a French passport. A cloak of official anonymity."

She studied him carefully, as if reevaluating him in light of this new information. "I had a client once. He'd been in the Legion. He told me the bond that forms between men with no allegiance to family or country or a past of any kind is formidable, close to mystical."

"It has to be," he said. "You die for each other, not a country."

"That's why you have the accent. And you've been rectified."

He nodded. "I did my five years. Jack Sauer became Jacques Sauvage—French citizen, perfectly legal."

"So that's how you got back into the country without tipping off the FBI, using the Sauvage alias?"

"No. I used a fake identity." He met her eyes. "And Sauvage *is* my name, not an alias."

"What happened after the five years?"

"I left the Legion with a couple of the guys I'd served with—Rafiq Zayed and Hunter McBride. Good guys— guys I'd kill for, and they for me."

"I don't doubt it," she whispered.

"We went to Africa where we were joined by a Zulu from South Africa, December Ngomo. He was ex-Umkhonto we Sizwe, the armed wing of the African National Congress established to fight the apartheid regime. We banded together to form a private military company." He sat back. "That was ten years ago. We call ourselves the Force du Sable."

"So you're shadow soldiers," she said softly. "Global cops for hire."

"Military advisors," he corrected. "Part of a growing multibillion-dollar industry. Wherever the next global hot spot flares into action, we're ready to step into the fray. For a fee. It's a legitimate business."

A haunted look sifted into her features. She dropped her face into her hands and sat like that for what seemed like ages. Then a silent sob racked her frame and he saw that her fingers were wet.

"Olivia?"

She jerked her head up, raw anguish in her eyes. "I *know* about the FDS, Jack!" Her voice was thick with hurt. "Your PMC is based on São Diogo Island off the coast of Angola. You were recently involved in a number of high-profile African coups, the protection of UN aid columns." She lurched to her feet, swayed slightly, steadied herself by holding onto the back of the sofa. "FDS troops helped end the civil war in Sierra Leone. They ousted a tyrannical dictator on the Ivory Coast, they've been instrumental in bringing an end to human genocide in a small Eastern European dictatorship. *I* know this, Jack." She jabbed her fingers into her chest. "I know it because *I've* dealt with clients from those areas. The FDS is lobbying for a United Nations sanction, forcing world leaders to rethink the role and legitimacy of mercenaries in a new world order. You want an international code of ethics."

"Yes," he said carefully. "We want to sift out the rogue operations. We want to make hiring a PMC a bankable option for small countries with limited military capability that might come under attack by a bigger hostile power."

She clutched her arms over her stomach, eyes burning with wet emotion. "I…I know all about your quest for legitimacy," she whispered. "I…I just didn't know it was *you*. All this time. You were alive and people were talking about you right there under my nose…my ex-fiancé…my dead fiancé…and I…you never… How could you *do* that to me, Jack? How could you not let me know you were all right?" She started to shake. "Damn you, Jack Sauer," she hissed, her eyes bright and wild. "Damn you all to hell."

"I've been there, Olivia."

"You should've stayed there." She swiped at the moisture on her face. "And now you're telling me President Elliot has hired the FDS? He's hired mercenaries to operate on U.S. soil, to come after my father and Grayson and some mysterious Cabal?"

"That's correct."

"But how did he hire you if he's supposed to be a virtual prisoner like you say he is?"

He studied her, his heart twisting, aching to comfort her. But he held his distance. This was good. She was asking the right questions. She was taking small steps to acceptance.

"It's a good question, Olivia," he said. "The only man President Elliot has been able to confide in is his private physician, Dr. Sebastian Ruger, an old and trusted military friend." Jacques wasn't going to go into the president's illness. Not yet. She wasn't ready for that.

"They've been communicating in writing, in the White House medical suite. The president asked Ruger to try to enlist us on his behalf. We've done work for him before, through a covert arm of the CIA, well before the Cabal managed to fully infiltrate the organization. He trusts us. Ruger managed to meet with me at a United Nations conference in Brussels just over three weeks ago. I was there to push my lobby for an international standardized code of conduct for private military companies." He paused. "It's a close-to-impossible mission, Olivia. But we took the job. Someone had to."

"You mean someone had to come after my father. And Grayson?"

"We're the last resort, Olivia, the last bid to save democracy. Because if your father and Forbes get their way, there won't be an election next month. Or for the foreseeable future. They'll immediately launch the country into a full-scale war with what they claim are terrorists and rogue states. This in turn will give Forbes unprecedented power, and he *will* use it. He will delay the election indefinitely and war will become his excuse to spark an era of aggressive imperialism expressly designed to feed corporate coffers—like those of your fathers. And this, Olivia, will change the world as we know it."

He let it sink over her.

She shook her head slowly. "You cannot," she said, "expect me to believe any of this. And even if some of it is remotely true, you cannot expect me to believe that my father is involved in anything like this."

"That's my job, then—to make you believe."

Defiance flashed in her eyes. "And if you can't?"

He looked pointedly at the cuff.

"Oh, right," she said bitterly. "You'll hold me hostage and threaten my father with my life?"

"Or you can choose to help us."

She glared at him. "My father is a good man, Jack. He…he may have some questionable ethics as far as business goes, but he is *not* involved in this. He can't be." But Jacques could see the nervousness, the edgy flickering questions in her eyes. Olivia knew just how connected and powerful her father was. She knew just how much Samuel Killinger craved power, how ruthless some of his business practices could be.

"It's not possible," she whispered, as if to convince herself. "He's a good man," she said again, quietly. "He could not do anything like this."

Jacques got to his feet, strode over to her floor-to-ceiling windows and flung back her drapes dramatically. He turned to face her, standing squarely in front of the black window…in full view of whoever was down in the street.

"What are you doing?"

"I'm going to show you something."

Confusion touched her eyes. The clock in the hall ticked loudly.

Olivia glanced at the clock. It was almost two in the morning. She'd be expected in the office by nine for a routine start. But there was *nothing* routine about this day. She fingered the smooth metal cuff he'd locked over her wrist, feeling as though she'd slid into some kind of twilight zone. She was unable to fully adjust to his presence, and she simply couldn't believe what he was telling her—especially about her father.

Jack had said the president had been ordered to stand down by October 13. Why did that date feel so familiar? She realized with mild shock that that was the day her father expected her to be on his yacht in the Caribbean for some big Venturion Corporation announcement. The whole board would be there. Her chest tightened. It was a coincidence. It *had* to be.

The familiar tone of her cell phone broke the silence. Olivia jumped, confused for a moment.

The chime sounded again.

Jack reached down, scooped her phone up from where he'd put it on the table, handed it to her. "Answer it." His eyes narrowed. "But remember, if *anyone* finds out I am in town, the bombs blow. People die."

She took the phone, flipped it open, checked the incoming number in the display. *Her father!* Tension whipped through her.

"Answer it."

She glanced at the clock again. Why on earth would her father be calling her at this hour?

She put the phone to her ear, her eyes fixed on Jack. "Dad?"

"Olivia, are you all right?"

No, I am not. Emotion choked her, stealing her voice.

"Olivia? You still there?"

"I…I'm fine, Dad."

Silence. "You don't sound fine."

She cleared her throat, shoved her hair back from her face as if it would help clear her mind. "I…I was sleeping."

Silence. Longer this time. He didn't believe her.

"Dad, do you know what time it is? Why are you calling me at this hour?"

"I was really worried about you, Olivia. I know Grayson was in town, and…and I hadn't heard from you. Did everything go okay? Did he propose?"

"What makes you think that?"

"It was on the news, the speculation."

She closed her eyes. It was not supposed to be like this.

"Did you accept, Olivia?"

"Dad, I…I can't talk now—"

"You're not alone…are you?"

Her eyes flared open. *He knew.* Somehow he knew.

Her eyes shot to Jack standing brazenly in front of the open curtains. She thought of the men in the street below watching.

That's how he knew!

Her heart bottomed out. They were her father's men outside. They were watching her window. He knew she had a man in her apartment tonight because they had called him. It was not a father's business. He had no right to spy on her like that. But why was he doing it? Why was he having her tailed? How long had she been followed?

A dark and sinister thread curled through her thoughts and nausea filled her stomach.

"Olivia?"

She swallowed against the growing thickness in her throat. "Dad…it's really late. I have to be up early. Can I call you back at a better time?"

"What happened with Grayson, Olivia?" His tone became insistent.

"I…" She watched Jack's eyes. "I've been meaning to break it off with him for some time, Dad. I was going to do it after he left office, when the pressure was off. But—"

"Grayson is good for you, Olivia. You're good to-gether." He hesitated. "Is…is there someone else? Is that the problem?"

Olivia felt ill. She knew what he was doing. He was pressing her for information—about the man in her window. And he was so desperate to know who that man was that he'd called her at this ungodly hour. Jack was right. Her father really *was* having her followed. Something *was* going on. Her world was crumbling out from under her feet and she couldn't even begin to think straight. Just seeing Jack, touching him, was more than she could handle right now.

Her voice began to choke up. "I...I have to go, Dad. I'll call you later." Olivia hung up quickly before he could speak again, and she stared numbly at the phone in her hand. She'd cut him off—her own father. She'd lied to him. *He'd* lied to *her.*

"I'm sorry, Olivia," Jack said softly. "I know this can't be easy."

Her eyes flashed to his. Well, if that wasn't the understatement of the night. Olivia sank back on to the sofa as she stared at Jack. He was the key in all this.

If what he said about the president was even vaguely true, why was *he* here, and not some other FDS operative?

It was because he knew her intimately. He understood the depth of her connection to her father. And he knew how to exploit that.

He also knew Grayson. They were all connected by the past.

A darkness whispered through her mind, an elusive sensation she couldn't quite pin down. Somehow...this tied back to Elizabeth's death, to that fateful night on the beach. She could sense it.

Whether she was right or not, it didn't matter. She needed to know. She needed to know this one thing before she could accept anything else that Jack said.

"Tell me, Jack," she said quietly. "Tell me what happened on the beach that night. I need to know why you killed Elizabeth."

"I didn't."

The brutal honesty in his voice slammed her square in the chest. She caught her breath, stared at him. His eyes were clear, unblinking. And with a sinking sensation, Olivia wondered if he might be telling the truth.

A dark question whispered, almost elusively, through her mind.

She tried to shake the thought away. And with a shock, she realized she'd been shaking that strange black whispering sensation away for longer than she cared to remember.

"If you didn't do it, Jack, who did?"

Chapter 4

02:47 Romeo. Olivia Killinger's apartment.
Manhattan. Wednesday, October 8.

He held her eyes for a long beat, the weight of the years and secrets stretching, hanging silent between them.

"I never wanted to go to that beach party," he said quietly. "They weren't my kind of people."

"Then why did you come?" She could feel herself being drawn down into the dark waters of her subconscious. And she could feel something swimming there, circling like a snake, something she couldn't quite grasp in the murk.

"I went for your sake. They were your friends, Olivia, and I loved you. I wasn't going to ask you to turn your back on the people you grew up with."

"If you loved me so much, Jack, why did you cheat on me?"

Something hard glittered in his eyes, but his voice remained level. "Let's stick to the facts, shall we. You were drunk that night, remember?"

That was part of her guilt, that she hadn't been fully aware of what had happened. That she couldn't recall little details, clues that might lie beyond the reach of her memory.

The horrible darkness crept closer to the surface. She began to feel edgy. Maybe she didn't want to hear what he had to say. Maybe she wanted it all to go away. Had she done that before? What if she had stuffed something down into her subconscious?

"So? Everyone was drinking," she said, her tone growing defensive now.

"I didn't drink that night. Do you remember that?"

She wasn't sure. She wasn't sure of anything about that night anymore. Especially not after the sessions with the therapist her father had made her see after the murder. The shrink had only made it murkier. Or had the weeks of sedatives done that? Or had she managed that all by herself?

"I wanted a clear head," he was saying. "I wanted to keep an eye out for you. There were drugs—some real weird stuff going around." He sat next to her and took her hands in his. He was so elegantly rugged. So strong. Always had been.

She'd loved him so much.

"Do you remember Forbes's advances, Olivia?"

She swallowed, nodded, noting how he refused to call him Grayson, always Forbes, holding him at bay.

"He was high. He came on to you early that evening, right in front of me, like he was trying to prove something, scrapping for a fight."

"Grayson always liked me, Jack. He always had a rivalry thing going with you."

His brow lowered sharply and his lip twitched. "When you told him to back off, Forbes turned in frustration to Elizabeth. Do you remember that part?"

She did. Vaguely.

"Liz and Forbes began to get hot and heavy right there by the fire, in front of everyone."

She slanted her eyes away from his, a strange nausea building in her stomach. Vague recollections of Grayson and Elizabeth swirled darkly in her memory. Her stomach tightened. "He…he didn't deny it, Jack. He told the police."

"What he *didn't* tell them, Olivia, is that Liz pulled herself together, pushed him off and took a walk down the beach to clear her head. She was cold, and I loaned her my jacket."

Her eyes whipped to his. *That would explain her blood, her DNA on your jacket. Why your jacket had been found with her body.*

"Forbes got up and followed her down the beach," he was saying.

Olivia closed her eyes, the sick darkness swirling tighter, tension mounting in her.

"I didn't like the look in Forbes's eyes. The guy's ego was wounded, and he was edgy, high, aggressive, sexually frustrated—a bad combination all-round." Jack

moved his thumb softly over the top her hand, and
Olivia's heart began to race wildly.

Part of her was ready to spring away from him.
Another part wanted to fold herself into him, feel his
hardness, his comfort, drink in his scent, bury her face
in his chest, hide…but from what? The truth? Why did
she feel this way? This is what she wanted, wasn't it?
Hadn't she wanted to look him in the eyes all these
years and ask him what really happened?

"The *only* mistake I made that night, Olivia—" his
lips were so close, his voice low, curling, twisting
through her "—was not going after him right away.
But when Liz didn't come back, I got worried. No
one else around the fire seemed to notice them missing—" he paused, looked at her pointedly "—includ-
ing you. So I went looking. I couldn't find her or
Forbes."

"And the next morning my cousin's body was discovered washed up on the beach, battered by waves, her
head fractured by a rock that was later found on the
beach with your jacket."

"Yes."

"And a witness said you were seen trying to force
yourself onto her."

"That witness being?"

Tension skidded toward panic. "Why would Grayson lie, Jack?"

"You tell me, Olivia."

"*No.* He would never—"

"And *I* would?"

Panic flared sharply. Memories, fears, repressed

questions began to whirl wildly in her brain. "What... what about that letter—Liz's letter, the one found in your jacket pocket? The one that indicated you'd been having a sexual relationship with her for months, that you wanted to marry me only for my money, that she was going to tell me if you didn't break it off with me?"

A look of incredulity, then anger sifted into his cool ice-gray eyes. "I can't believe you bought that. It was typed on the same kind of paper stocked in Elizabeth's printer, but it wasn't Liz who wrote that letter. I'd never seen it before in my life."

"You saying it was *planted?* By who? Who could have had access to your jacket? It was…evidence."

His eyes held hers. "Your father was well connected, Olivia."

"Oh, some cop or some CSI guy planted it? Get real, Jack." She jerked free of his hold, fighting back the dark sensations inside her, fighting to move away from his absorbing presence, from the implications of what he was saying. "My father had *nothing* to do with that investigation!"

Anger pulsed through his neck. He got to his feet, glared down at her, his voice dangerously level. "Samuel Killinger just *happened* to hire an army of top criminal lawyers, did he? He just *happened* to need regular meetings with the lead investigators and the D.A.? His lawyers just *happened* to brief Grayson Forbes *before* he was questioned by police, and then just *happened* to be present when he was?"

Dread tightened like a noose, and fear hummed through her body. "If…if you really are innocent, why did you run? Why…why didn't you let them take you in? Why didn't you stand trial—"

"Against all the crooked evidence and legal corruption a fortune can buy?" His eyes sparked. "Are you nuts? Your father's connections and influence make the Mafia look like child's play, and I was the kid from the wrong side of the tracks." Anger burned into his features, and powered his voice. "Did you never ask yourself, Olivia, why your father was paying lawyers in the first place?"

"Liz was his sister's child. My aunt was a single mother. She was completely crushed and incapacitated by what happened. My dad *had* to do something."

"Yeah, he did something all right. He used me as a scapegoat. He used Lizzie's murder to get me out of your life. For good."

"That's not true!"

He snorted. "Think about it, Olivia." he tapped his temple. "How would it have looked on the national news networks—Senator Forbes's son guilty of murder? The famous senator was supported by the entire Venturion Corporation board, and your father personally. His son, Grayson Forbes, Jr., was already being groomed by your father's men—the *Cabal*—for the highest office in the nation." His eyes burned into hers like ice fire.

She backed further into the sofa.

He pointed his finger at her. "There was more than one political future at stake that night, Olivia. Even your father's reputation was at risk. And given what we know about the Cabal now, there is no way in hell Samuel Killinger was going to tolerate reporters sniffing around the Venturion board members and their connections to the Senate and Congress—they were already at work on their plan to take over the government back then."

She felt truly ill. She didn't want to believe it. But in a small part of her brain he was making sense. Absurd sense, but sense.

His voice lowered further, growing more sinister. "Your father wanted to see you in the White House even back then, Olivia. And for that it was necessary for you to marry Forbes. Not me—not some left-wing radical roughneck who stood against his global corporate philosophies. He wanted me gone. Forever. And he wanted Forbes in. He found the perfect opportunity. And the perfect scapegoat."

Olivia got to her feet and pushed past him. She needed space. She crossed to the middle of the room, closer to the door, then she spun to face him. "That's just sick, Jack. He'd never use Lizzie's death for something like that." But her voice sounded hollow, defeated. "There…there is just no way my father would want me to marry a guy he knew was guilty of murder."

He angled his head. "You so sure?"

She suddenly wasn't so sure. Of anything. "You're trying to tell me that the vice president of this country is guilty of homicide? Do you realize what kind of effect that accusation could have?"

"Oh, so you think *I* should take the rap instead?"

She stared at him blankly.

"Is that what your father managed to convince you

to do all those years ago, Olivia? Turn on the man you loved because of the political implications?"

"That's not true and you know it."

"Sure looks that way from where I stand."

She couldn't breathe. She couldn't seem to order the information spinning in her head. "Is that why you're back now, Jack? For some kind of revenge? You want to hurt the people you believe hurt you?"

His face darkened to thunder, the movement twisting his scar viciously. "Call it revenge, retribution or call it justice if you want—however it comes, I'm going to take it, Olivia. You're damn right on that count." He was really angry now. "*You* of all people should relate to the concept of justice. But that is *not* why I'm back. I'm here because I have a job to do. I'm here because I know how to get to your father. Quickly. Quietly. And efficiently."

"Through me."

"Through you."

"You came back for him, not me." Why she said it, she didn't know. But it mattered to say. It hurt.

She felt as if she was being ripped in two. He was calling her a hypocrite. He was accusing her of injustice, betrayal. He was accusing the people in her life of…she suddenly felt dirty. She had a desperate need to wash it all away.

"I…I need a shower." She put out her wrist. "Take this thing off."

"It's waterproof, shockproof. You can shower, you can do what the hell you like with it. Just can't take it off."

"Dammit, Jack, please take it off." *Please make this all go away.*

"Olivia, I can't trust you." His eyes were cold. "I don't know how involved in this you may be, and I don't know what kind of hold your father still has over you."

"That's absurd! You can't think—"

"Look what happened sixteen years ago. Look who you believed back then. Look at how much trouble you're having believing me now."

She fell silent. How could she begin to explain what had been going on in her head back then, when she didn't even understand it herself. Not even now."

"And you are *still* in a position to be first lady, if your father succeeds, if you change your mind and accept Forbes's proposal."

"I told you," she whispered, "I turned him down."

"You *are* still wearing his ring," he said, and turned his back on her. He stalked to the window, stared out over the dark city.

He looked so alone. Powerful but alone. What had he endured all these years? How much of a part had she played in his pain? Unwittingly? Because she would never, *ever* have hurt him intentionally. She loved him too much. Pain so raw and sharp spilled through her and burned at her eyes.

"Jack…it wasn't like that, it wasn't like you say."

He said nothing.

"Please, Jack, please look at me."

"How was it, then?" He asked, still facing the window. "When exactly did you stop believing in me, Olivia? Why did you not want to at least listen to my side?"

"Because you never gave me a chance," she said, her eyes brimming with tears. "You fled."

"Bull." He whirled round. "I tried to see you. I tried to talk to you. But your butler, your servants, they all treated me like some third-rate citizen. They wouldn't let you take my calls. They wouldn't even let me enter the gates to your property!"

"I…I didn't know."

"You didn't know much, did you, Olivia?"

"I…I was nineteen, Jack. I was absolutely devastated by Lizzie's death. And when they said you were a person of interest in her murder—the lawyers, the cops, they *instructed* me not to speak to you. My dad had me sedated…" As she spoke, she felt sicker, the realization drawing on her that he might have been manipulated in some way.

"Go on."

"You…you left before they could take you into custody, before I could say goodbye." The tears spilled over her cheeks. "And then you went and *died* on me." She wiped her eyes. "Tell me, what was left for me to do then? Apart from try to forget. You were gone!"

Pain pulled at his face, twisted his scar.

She sniffed, rubbed her nose. "I would have come, Jack. If you had found a way to let me know you were still alive, I would have come to you. In Alaska. In Russia. In France, Africa, wherever…*I would have come*."

His jaw clenched. "Why? Why would you have come if you thought I was guilty?"

"To ask you why you'd done it! To hear it from your lips. To look into your eyes when you told me. And maybe, Jack, maybe you could have spared us all by telling me the truth back then." She held his gaze from across the room. "Maybe our world would be a very different place right now. Maybe there would be no Vice President Grayson Forbes, and just maybe there would be no biological threat hanging over our nation. Have you thought about *that?*"

She was shaking so hard she could barely stand. She turned, headed to her bedroom, closed the door behind her, locked it with trembling fingers. She stared at the lock through the tears streaming down her face.

Jack stared at the door.

She'd have come? To him? To Africa, Europe? What could have been…

He sat heavily in the chair. Sick. A lifetime wasted. He pinched the bridge of his nose, trying to cut the pain in his head. He couldn't. He heard the shower go on. He thought of Olivia, naked, apart from the cuff…and Forbes's ring. He launched to his feet, marched across the room, poured a whiskey, sucked it back sharply. And he felt rage fire into his heart.

He clenched the glass, too tightly. He was going to kill the man who'd done this to them. He was going to rip Killinger into shreds with his bare hands. He was going to do it before the week was out.

And then he'd start on Forbes.

He slammed the glass down, inhaled sharply, squared his shoulders. Maintaining control was imperative for the success of this mission. That was why he was here.

Yes, he had to deal with the past. And yes, he had to

go through this process with Olivia. And yes, it was as damned personal as it could ever get.

But that was precisely why he had been the unquestionable choice for this phase of the mission. His emotional connection to Olivia Killinger was a tool. And he had no choice but to use that tool.

He walked slowly back to the window and looked into the streets of Manhattan. A pale-gray dawn would soon be leaching into the sky. A new day.

And the clock was still ticking.

He reached for his sat phone, punched in McDonough's number, cleared his throat. "You still receiving the GPS signal?"

"Affirmative."

"Good. She's in the shower, and it's still working."

"What do you want us to do about her tail?"

"Nothing. We use them."

"How?"

"We make Killinger think his daughter is seeing another man, other than Forbes. It could flush him out, make him do something rash." He checked his watch. "Does the Devilliers cyber litter check out okay?"

"Affirmative."

"We stick with that alias, then. She's probably going to try and make a run for it sometime this morning. I'm going to let her go, give her a bit of space to work things out. Keep close. Let me know her movements. And monitor any calls she makes, cell or landline. I want to know who she contacts and what she says."

"Will do."

"You got any news on December?"

There was a slight hesitation. "He's still critical, on life support."

Jacques swore. "Keep me posted. Achromat talking yet?" he asked, referring to the albino man who'd tracked Zayed and wounded December in Hamān as they'd brought the scientist out just three days ago—the scientist who'd unwittingly created the biological monstrosity, a variation of which was now contained in a vial on Olivia's wrist. Jacques figured the man was somehow connected to Killinger, but there was something more about him. He felt like pure evil embodied.

"*Nothing* has made him talk. That guy is not human, I swear."

"There's always something to make someone talk. Tell the guys to keep at it." He signed off.

December Ngomo was a loyal comrade. He'd saved Jacques's life on more than one occasion. Jacques owed him.

He owed them all.

This was why his resolve, his focus must stay firmly on the mission.

He listened for the water in the bathroom. He could still hear it. He felt for the box in his pocket, set it on the table, opened it carefully.

The indention in the black velvet designed to hold the cuff was empty. Next to it was a silver rectangle, a little smaller in shape than a military dog tag, a couple of millimeters thicker. A sealed vial and syringe nestled beside it—the detonator and the antidote.

Jacques extracted the silver slab, held it in the palm of his hand, studied it. If he flipped the top of the tab open and pressed the electronic pad inside, a remote signal would activate an impulse in the cuff that would shoot a needle right into Olivia's arm and release the lethal pathogen into her system. It was effective up to a hundred yards away.

In his hand he now held the power to destroy her, just at a press of a button, just as her father held the power to destroy a nation.

Killinger would understand this kind of logic. And he certainly knew the potential of this particular pathogen. It was fitting, thought Jacques, as he placed the detonator carefully back into the case, that the same biological bullet aimed at the heart of the country was now aimed right at his daughter.

He closed the box, slipped it back into his pocket. How easy, he wondered, would it be to be walk the fine line between pretending to be Olivia's lover and wanting to be?

And just where did that line begin and end? Because it was already blurred to hell and gone in his head. He figured he'd crossed it once already.

And when the crunch did come, how easy was it going to be for him to press that detonator?

How far would Killinger go for absolute power? And how far would *he* go to stop him?

He could not allow his desire for a woman to cause the downfall of the nation.

Chapter 5

04:59 Romeo. Olivia Killinger's apartment.
Manhattan. Wednesday, October 8.

Olivia stepped out of the shower, wiped the steam from the mirror and stared at the silver bracelet. She yanked at it again, trying to force it over her wrist, but there was no way she could get it off, even with wet skin.

In frustration she curled her fingers around the Saint Catherine's pendant and angrily tore the thin gold chain from her neck, dropping it onto the edge of the basin. *Damn Jack!*

She wrenched off the diamond ring Grayson had given her and plunked it on top of the chain. She didn't belong to either of them.

Wrapping herself in a robe, Olivia padded through

her bedroom and listened at the door. Jack was still in her apartment and it sounded as though he was banging things around in her kitchen.

She glanced at the phone next to her bed. No, using her cell would be better. He couldn't pick up and listen in. She could call the FBI.

But what if he really was telling the truth?

Olivia sank down onto her bed, cell phone in hand, wet hair dripping, and started to shake all over again. *Jack was back. He was alive.*

Her eyes burned.

She lifted her face to the ceiling and sucked in a breath. God, how she wanted to believe he was innocent…that he really never meant to hurt or betray her.

But believing in his innocence raised too many questions, things she was afraid to even think about, things that had been buried too deep for too long. But his return was forcing her to dig into her soul, to confront herself and the past she desperately wanted to forget.

Olivia didn't want to find out that she was responsible in some way for what had happened to him. The guilt would be unbearable.

What if she hadn't listened to the lawyers or the cops all those years ago? What if she'd refused the sedatives her father's doctor had given her right after Elizabeth's death? What if she'd kept her mind clear, hadn't gone through hypnosis with that awful therapist? What if she'd defied them all and gone to find him instead, and asked *him* what had happened?

What would Jack have done if the situation was reversed?

He would have come to her. That's the kind of guy he was.

She'd let him down. She should have gone to him, heard his side of the story. Instead she'd trusted the voice of authority and the system rather than listen to the whispers of doubt in her heart.

And then he was gone—dead—and it was too late.

Why had she not admitted these things to herself before? Why had she not faced these questions before?

If Jack was telling the truth it would mean her entire life had been a farce. It would mean her father had intentionally deceived her. It would mean Grayson had made love to her knowing he had killed her cousin, knowing he had destroyed her fiancé, taken the most precious thing from her life.

She thought about her father's odd phone call, about the gathering planned for the yacht on the thirteenth, about the strange timing of Grayson's out-of-the-blue proposal, and nausea rode through her stomach.

No. She *had* to stop this. She had to deal in facts, not crazy emotions. As a lawyer, she never made decisions until she had enough proof, so why should she do any different now?

Why *should* she believe Jack off the bat? He hadn't contacted her in sixteen years—why now? He was using her—he'd said so. And if he had reason to use her, he had motive to bend the truth.

She'd be a complete fool to trust him.

Olivia stood up pushed her damp hair back from her face. Facts. Clarity. That's what she needed.

The first thing she was going to do was check him

out—everything he'd said. She was going to see if she could confirm his involvement with the FDS. She was going to find out what her UN connections knew about the organization…anything she could lay her hands on. And she was going to keep moving forward, gathering as many facts as she could. She'd think afterward, she'd decide how to feel later.

He said they had six days.

Olivia began to pace up and down her bedroom, adrenaline rising as she thought, plotted. She checked her clock. Pria wouldn't be in the office this early. She'd have to wait.

She lifted her wrist, examined the bracelet again. Could it be a hoax? Did it really have a GPS in it? She turned her wrist over. There was no sign of it. What did she know? She wouldn't have a clue what such a device looked like anyway.

She could test it. She could find a way to sneak out and see if he came running.

She stilled.

Yes, that's what she had to do. She needed to go to Venturion Tower. She wanted to look into her father's eyes, and ask him some careful questions about the past.

She wanted to see his warm smile and know that he could not have anything to do with this alleged coup plot.

She began to pace again. Damn Jack. He'd driven a razor's edge of doubt right through her soul. He was making her question her own father. Well, she wasn't going to, not without proof.

Olivia yanked open her closet door, and found herself selecting a silk shirt in a color that had once been Jack's favorite on her—a soft champagne. She held the fabric against her skin, a memory rustling softly through her mind—of a dress she'd once had in the same color. He'd said it offset her eyes, made them the color of liquid honey, that it had accentuated the copper highlights in her chestnut hair.

She cursed softly, tossed the shirt on the bed, took another out. This one was a rich emerald-green silk, a solid, bold, strong color—one that exuded confidence. Because *that's* how she was determined to feel—confident, in control, just like she was in the courtroom.

She chose her pants carefully, going for cream, neatly tailored, with a small zipper in the back and a wide flare at the bottom that gave her movements an elegant fluidity when she walked. Olivia knew how to project image. It was part of what made her a success. She could look poised even when insecurity was eating her alive.

She dressed, took stock in the mirror, and decided to wear her hair clipped back. She added a mere slick of pale gloss to her lips but lined her eyes carefully with dark kohl. The darkness offset the gold color, made them look lighter, almost predatory. She stood back and assessed her reflection. She didn't look the victim anymore, even if Jack was trying to play her as one, even if she was his prisoner with this damn handcuff on her wrist.

Satisfied, Olivia sucked in a breath and proceeded to unlock the door.

* * *

Jack whipped eggs with all the controlled violence of a caged wild animal. He added pepper, salt, a dash of Tabasco and a splash of milk. It splattered right over the edge of the bowl and onto his pants. He muttered a curse, grabbed one of Olivia's dishcloths and tucked it into his waistband.

The espresso steamed from the coffee machine, and milk frothed. He'd already tossed a handful of button mushrooms into the frying pan where they hissed and popped.

The shower had gone off ages ago, but Olivia was still in the bedroom. Was she going to hide in there all day?

He opened her fridge and caught sight, again, of the photograph of her and Grayson, stuck to the door with a sunflower fridge magnet.

He reached in and grabbed a tomato, too hard, sinking his finger into the soft innards. He swore, plopped his finger in his mouth, sucked the juice off as he turned and kicked the door shut with his heel.

And there she was. Beautiful and poised in dark-emerald silk.

He went stock-still, finger still in his mouth, a mutilated tomato in his fist, juice running down his wrist, suddenly feeling awkward at the compromising position he found himself in. He slid the finger slowly out of his mouth.

She swallowed, watching his lips.

He could see sexual interest in her eyes. She tried to control it, couldn't. *Wow*. Those eyes looked like they belonged to a hungry lioness. And the effect was a punch to his gut.

He caught his breath, pulled himself together, ripped his gaze away, set the mangled tomato on a board, picked up a knife.

"Hungry?" he asked raising the knife.

She watched the blade slice into the fruit, slid her eyes up to meet his. "No."

He held his breath again for an instant, trying to acclimate himself to the power of her eyes all made up like that, to the latent confidence that simmered in them. She had gone into the shower one woman, and she'd come out quite another. Granted, she'd taken her time, but he had to hand it to her.

Or not.

Careful, Jack, she could be playing you.

He stilled suddenly. He'd just thought of himself as Jack! This was not good. He wanted to dig into the past but he'd had zero intention of delving that far back into his psyche. It was her—*she* was doing this to him.

His heart raced softly, but outwardly he stayed nonchalant. "You need to eat," he said. "I've made some breakfast."

Her eyes lowered to the dishcloth in his pants, and a hesitant lightness flickered over her lips.

He held his hands out to his side, knife in one. "What? I look funny?"

"It's the sunflower print," she said, a hint of mirth in her voice. "They look so…innocent." She cleared her throat. "They don't quite go with the gun you have tucked in the back of your pants."

The idea of a smile crossed his mind but didn't quite make it to his lips. "You have a thing for sunflowers, don't you?" He said, turning back to the tomato, thinking of the photo on the fridge. He smacked the knife down on the board. "Feel better in combat gear myself," he said.

She watched him scrape what was now tomato mush into the pan. "So you still like to cook, Jack?"

A memory whispered through him, of cooking for Olivia, of making love in front of the fire. "No, not unless it's on a campfire in the bush. Usually someone cooks for me."

"A woman?"

She held his gaze, direct, challenging. She really had pulled herself together back there. This was the Olivia he could imagine in a courtroom.

"There's no woman in my life," he said.

She looked him over again, even more slowly this time. "No woman? You're kidding me."

He hesitated. He didn't want to go there, didn't have to, but it came out anyway. "Hasn't been a woman for…a long time."

"How long?"

"Too long."

"You telling me you don't have sex, Jack?"

Surprise flickered through him. He studied her face, trying to read where she was going with this. Silence grew taut, just the sizzle of mushrooms and tomato in the pan. "I didn't say that, now, did I?" he turned, picked up a fork, quickly sautéed the contents of the pan. He was conscious of her watching his hands—hands that were far more familiar around an AK-47 or machete than a kitchen paring knife.

"So you sleep with them but don't care about them, is that what you're implying?"

The muscles in his back tightened. He turned slowly to face her, and his eyes collided with hers again. "There was only one woman I cared about, Olivia. I learned the hard way what that kind of caring can do to a man. It's not worth it. I don't bother, not anymore."

She paled visibly. "So, you have superficial relationships, and that's—"

"That's about it. Yeah. What is it with these questions? You going to continue down this road or what?"

"You asked *me* if I loved Grayson."

His eyes flicked to her hand. She wasn't wearing the ring. His pulse kicked up softly. Then he saw that she wasn't wearing his pendant, either.

She was making a statement. She wasn't taking sides.

Well, it was his job to make her do that. And cooking her breakfast, endearing himself to her, was part of the plan.

He picked up the egg mixture, poured it into the pan.

"You know," she said, as she watched him folding the egg into the tomato and mushrooms. "I don't get you, Jack." She waved her hand around the kitchen. "I don't get any of this. You walk back into my life after sixteen years, you ask me if I love the man who has just proposed to me, and *then* you inform me that he and my father are going to overthrow the U.S. Government." Her voice hitched slightly, betraying her show of confidence. "And then you come in here, like…like some gladiator in a dishcloth and dress pants, and you make me breakfast?"

Her eyes began to glisten, but she turned away quickly, trying to hide it from him.

He reached out, touched her shoulder. "Livie—" he said softly.

She stiffened under his hand.

"Livie, look at me."

"Don't—" she said, her back still to him. "Do not call me that again."

"Okay, I won't, but—" The toast caught, and acrid smoke burned into the air. He swore, lurched over the counter, flicked the toaster switch up and knocked an egg off the counter in the process. It smashed to the floor.

He cursed again, took the frying pan off the heat, reached for a cloth, dropped to his haunches and started mopping up the slippery mess. She just stood there watching him. What was it about kitchens and beautiful women that could make a man feel so inadequate?

"It does that," she said.

He glanced up from his position on the floor. "Does what?"

"The toaster. You have to put it on a lower heat than usual."

"Next time."

She leaned over him, grabbed two more slices of bread, adjusted the toaster thermostat and shunted the lever down. "There won't be a next time."

He got to his feet, cornering her between himself and the exit. "Sure there'll be a next time."

She swallowed, her eyes suddenly nervous.

"We're going to be spending a good deal of time together these next few days, Olivia. You better get used to it."

He reached across her, catching her fragrance as he did. He grabbed the pan, slid the omelet onto a plate on the counter, and pushed it toward her. "Eat. Then join me in your study."

"Why?"

"I need your computer. I have to show you something. And you're not going to want to eat after you see it."

Olivia stepped out of the kitchen and into the hallway. He was busy in her study, off the end of the living room. She was out of his line of sight. She could leave, right now, just walk out that door. She stared at her own front door, fingers clenching and unclenching at her sides, a prickle of perspiration forming on her upper lip. She really should go. Now. And it could all be over.

But she couldn't. She'd be deluding herself. Something was going on and she was now committed to finding out what it was. She needed the truth. She wasn't going to stick her head in the sand again. Ever.

Facts, Olivia, get the facts. Keep yourself emotionally zipped up until you have them all. Then act. Control yourself. You can do this....

She made herself move across the living room, and she cautiously pushed open the study door.

His back was to her. He was bent over some kind of PDA, busy connecting it to her system, his shoulder muscles moving smoothly under his white shirt. She figured he must have had the shirt tailored to fit his extra powerful frame, because the fit was exquisite.

"You eat?"

The question startled her.

He glanced up, the morning light catching his eyes. Her stomach tightened. God, he was gorgeous. Grim, but gorgeous.

"Well, did you?"

"Yes."

"Food okay?"

It was damn good, but she wasn't about to tell him that.

"Forget the small talk, Jack. How come you're letting me walk around like this if you're so worried about this coup threat? I could have gone right out my door. I could have left—"

"I know where you are with that bracelet. I told you, it has a GPS. Sit. You need to see this."

Damn him, he could be frustrating.

"I've linked a satellite feed to your system." He tapped some keys, and the monitor sprung to life.

She seated herself, keeping as much space as she could between them. His energy was just too consuming to get too close. But he yanked her chair up against his, forcing her arm to brush against his where he'd rolled up his sleeves. A frisson of heat shivered over her skin. She swallowed. "What have you got?"

His eyes flicked quickly down her cleavage and back to her face, something wicked dancing in them for all of a nanosecond. Then he turned back to the computer, hit a key, then leaned back in his chair and watched her watch.

An image filled her screen. It was some kind of military field hospital in a jungle clearing. Patients were lining up, getting injections. She couldn't see any faces, just arms, hands, latex gloves, snatches of camouflage gear. Her interest piqued instantly, and she leaned forward to get a better look.

It looked like some kind of army vaccine program. Somewhere in central Africa, judging by the equatorial vegetation and the blood-red soil.

Her screen filled with another image—patients sitting on cots, emaciated, bleeding from the nose and mouth. Her heart quickened. Then there was another shot, different time sequence, of the same patients thrashing wildly, attacking each other, tearing flesh, biting, drawing blood, salivating.

Her hand shot to her mouth. "Oh my God! What *is* this?"

"That's four days after initial infection."

Olivia felt the blood drain from her head. "Why are they attacking each other like that?"

"The pathogen eats into their brains, causing rapid dementia and triggering a violent aggression in its host. It's the way the disease spreads itself, through blood, saliva and other bodily fluids."

The next image to fill her screen was of men and women, eyes rolled back into their heads, cut, scratched, bitten, bleeding from every orifice, twitching and writhing in what looked like excruciating pain. They were shackled to the cots with leather belts and canvas straps.

"That's after six days."

A strange noise escaped her chest.

In the next clip men in black hazmat suits were rolling bodies into a massive pit dug out of the red soil. They then poured what looked like lime over the corpses. The final clip was the entire camp being razed by fire, black smoke boiling into the jungle air.

Her eyes shot to his in horror.

"Seven days from start to finish," he said. "Very violent, very painful, and very, very frightening."

"What is this, Jack? What is that disease?"

"That—" he pointed to the screen "—is what'll happen in New York, Chicago and Los Angeles in six days or less. That, Olivia, is the digital footage that was sent to President Elliot, showing him what will happen right here in the United States if he does not step down and relinquish his leadership by midnight, October 13."

"Where was this! Where did this happen?"

"Near Ishonga, in Congo-Brazzaville."

"Up near the Shilongwe River?"

"Not far from the Gabonese border. You're familiar with the area?"

"Yes, I am. Civil war is rife in that region. There have been allegations of genocide. The place is a complete mess. No one really knows what goes on in there."

"The perfect place for illegal clinical trials of a genetically engineered pathogen, given under the guise of a vaccine program, wouldn't you say?"

She narrowed her eyes at the screen. Her brain was working in overdrive now. Her heart was beating so fast she could barely breathe. Injustices like this drove her wild. It was the reason she worked for the UN, why she did what she did for a living. "How do you know it's the Ishonga region?"

"We didn't, not initially. But see here—" he clicked the mouse, took the footage back to the initial frame where vaccines were being given. He froze the image, enlarged it several times and pointed. "We digitally enhanced the footage. See in that far corner? See that maroon beret, and that glimpse of an armband there? That's the uniform of People's Militia. It pointed us straight to the Congo-Brazzaville region."

She glanced at the silver cuff on her wrist, at the pale gold capsule in the window. Panic licked at her. "Is…is the same disease in *this* capsule?"

He hesitated.

She lurched to her feet. "Is it the same, Jack!"

"It has a small genetic variation, but yes, basically it is the same."

She stared at him in sheer horror. He might be Jack Sauer, but this man was a complete stranger to her.

"Olivia—" he reached to touch her arm "—I'm sorry."

She jerked away. "You bastard," she whispered. "How could you?"

He got to his feet slowly. "If you want to blame someone for that disease, Olivia—" his eyes drilled into hers "—blame your father, not me."

Chapter 6

07:40 Romeo. Olivia Killinger's apartment.
Manhattan. Wednesday, October 8.

"Oh no." She shook her head. "You're not saying that—"

"That he created that monster? That he orchestrated those trials on innocent villagers? That's exactly what I'm saying."

"He couldn't!"

"Not personally, Olivia, but he pulled all the strings. He had the pathogen isolated and genetically modified at Nexus—a highly secretive offshore lab indirectly owned by one of his subsidiaries and operated in the Sultanate of Hamān—specifically to avoid U.S. over-sight. The scientist who did the work is Dr. Paige Ster-

ling. She isolated the causative agent of a previously un-
known prion disease peculiar to a rare troop of pygmy
chimps found exclusively in the Blacklands region of
the Congo. She made a breakthrough that defies current
scientific thinking. Her work has enabled the creation
of a whole new generation of prion illnesses."

He paused. "We have Dr. Sterling now. We brought
her out of Hamān three days ago. She's helping manu-
facture antidote in a level-four lab we've set up on São
Diogo."

"She's *helping* you?"

"She didn't know how her work was being used to
this end, Olivia. Paige Sterling and her parents were
basically owned and manipulated by Venturion organizations, namely Science Reach International and the
Nexus Research and Development Group."

Dismay clouded her eyes. She slowly sat again.

"We don't yet know how your father plans to deliver
this bioweapon, Olivia, but we suspect it has been made
airborne and packed into some form of explosive device. Dr. Sterling showed us it can be done."

She stared blankly at the screen, her focus distant.

"Can you imagine what you saw on this screen happening right here in New York? It will be pure terror,
and only a matter of time before it becomes a pandemic.
This is not a virus, Olivia, and it's not a bacteria. Doc-
tors around the world will *not* be able to stop this without access to Dr. Sterling's work or the antidote."

"Why, Jack, why would my father be involved in something like this? It doesn't make sense. What good would
a pandemic do him?" she asked without looking at him.

"BioMed Pharmaceutical will market the antidote. BioMed will hold the patent."

"And BioMed is a Venturion subsidiary?" she said quietly.

"Yes, Venturion stands to gain financially, and the Cabal will be able to coordinate, manipulate and contain the outbreak, to a degree. But there will still be vast loss of life. We've located some of the antidote stockpiles offshore, but we haven't moved in on them yet, because we cannot tip our hand without tipping off your father. That alone would trigger the release of the pathogen. In the meantime, we are manufacturing as much antidote as we can on São Diogo under Dr. Sterling's direction."

She looked up at him. "How did *you* get samples of the disease? From Dr. Sterling?"

She was thinking the logic through. This was good. He was making progress. But he wasn't going to tell her all of it yet. There was only so much she was going to be able to absorb in one day.

"We got the pathogen from a nurse who fled Ishonga with tissue samples from infected villagers. The disease managed to escape the trial group and ended up at a small mission clinic. Cabal-controlled militia moved in to destroy the mission compound and everything in it, but the nurse got away. We intercepted her distress call. We were monitoring communications in that region after seeing this footage. Hunter McBride brought her out."

She swallowed, looking as if she might faint.

"Can I get you some water, Olivia, or something else to drink?"

She shook her head, stood up, went to the window, looked down into the street. He noticed she was twisting the bracelet round and round and round her wrist.

He came to her side. "I'll bet my life that those guys down there are carrying the antidote with them, just in case your father is forced to release the bombs. They probably have orders and the means to get you out of the country ASAP if things go sideways."

She said nothing.

He cupped her jaw, turned her face, making her look at him. "Your father wants you to be safe, Olivia. He loves you, and that's why he's tailing you."

"And this?" She held out her arm with the cuff. "Do they have the antidote to *this* variation?"

He hesitated. "No. Your father's antidote will not work on that."

A small shudder ran through her body. She moved away from him and covered her stomach with her arms. The hurt of betrayal in her eyes was profound, and it tore at his gut.

"You say this thing is going to happen in six days, if the president doesn't stand down?"

"If you don't help us stop it."

She stood silent for several minutes, staring into the street.

"And if the president *does* stand down?"

She wasn't ready to learn that it wouldn't end there, that it would just be the beginning.

"He won't, Olivia. We *have* to stop your father." He touched her shoulder. She tensed, moved away.

"I don't buy it," she said. "Why do you need me? If

my father is this…this ogre you say he is, why don't you just go get him yourselves?"

"We can't. His security is excellent. If he gets so much as a whiff that we are on to him, those bombs *will* blow." Jack paused. "And if we try and take him down and he gets killed, those bombs could be programmed to go off anyway. He would have built in some kind of insurance policy for himself. He alone has to stop this. You *have* to get me close to him, Olivia. You have to get me into that inner sanctum of his, and together we must make *him* pull the plug."

She bit her bottom lip.

"It's the only way, Olivia…unless you want me to use the bracelet."

Her eyes flashed hotly to his. "How does the bracelet work?"

He considered her carefully, decided to play it straight. He took hold of her wrist, turned it over. "See that—" he pointed to a fine join in the silver "—the hinge is in there. The cuff locks at the underside here," he said turning her arm. "If you open it without the de-activation key, it will create pressure on that hinge, and that in turn will fire an impulse—a microscopic explosion—which will force a needle into your arm and feed the solution from the capsule directly into your system."

Still holding her hand in his, he looked into her eyes. "You'll start to bleed internally almost immediately. Death will take a while longer."

Her skin went sheet white. "And if you cut through the metal, without putting pressure on the hinge?"

"There's an electronic thread that runs through the

core of the metal. If severed, it will trigger the same impulse. Same result."

She withdrew her hand slowly, a look of hatred and disbelief leaking into her golden eyes.

"Olivia," he said slowly, "I *want* to trust you. And more than anything in this world I want you to trust *me*."

Her eyes narrowed as she peered deep and hard into his. "Jack," her voice was flat, strangely devoid of emotion, "I would never condone anything like you've shown me in that footage. It goes against everything I am, everything I've worked for. If any of this is true, which I'm having trouble accepting right now, then I *will* do what is in my power to stop it."

"Then, Olivia, I must prove to you it is true." He watched her eyes. "And you must prove to me that you will take my word over your father's. You must show me that your belief in justice runs thicker than your blood."

A teensy stress muscle began to pulse at the corner of her eye. He ached to place his fingers over it, to tell her it would be all right, if she just trusted him. But she turned her back on him, walked smoothly, calmly to the bedroom and shut the door softly behind her.

Once again Jack heard the twist of the lock, and he felt his heart twist with it.

Olivia double-checked the door was locked. Then she went into the bathroom, shut that door and locked it, too. She sat on the edge of the tub clutching her cell phone in her hands and she tried to think. But she couldn't. Her mind had gone blank. And when she looked at her watch again she was shocked to see how long she'd been sitting there totally numb. It was almost nine in the morning and she'd be expected at the office any minute. Her heart quickened. She had to do something.

Olivia glanced at the bathroom door, half expecting him to break two sets of locks and barge right in. He'd managed to walk into her apartment, back into her life and right back into her soul. She wouldn't put anything past him right now.

She hit the quick-dial to her office, tension prickling over her scalp as the phone rang and rang at the other end. Her assistant finally picked up.

"Hi, Pria." Olivia forced lightness into her voice. "I just wanted to let you know that I won't be coming into the office for the next few days."

"Olivia? Are you okay? Anything wrong?"

She laughed lightly, falsely, hand tight on the phone. "No, no, everything's fine," she lied. "It's just that I've had some...personal matters come up that need to be dealt with right away." *Like national security. Like a dead fiancé coming back to life. Like my father being accused of trying to overthrow the country.* She felt herself wobble at the enormity of what lay in front of her. She took a deep breath, controlled her voice. "I am going to be doing some work from home, however, and I was hoping you could patch me through to Harvey? He should be in the building today."

Harvey was a Brit of Asian descent, a techno-geek genius who worked on several systems at UN headquarters. He was also a friend, someone she'd helped out when his parents had run into serious immigration problems. It was time to call in the favor.

Pria had Harvey on the line within minutes.

"Hey, Olivia, what's up?"

Perspiration began to bead on her forehead. She eyed the door again, lowered her voice. "I need a favor, Harv, a big one. I'll compensate you for your time."

"Don't be ridiculous. Where are you, I can barely hear you?"

She glanced at the door again. "Just bad reception. I…I'll speak up."

"That's better. What can I do for you?"

"I'm working on…on a case. It's convoluted, highly sensitive. I'd prefer not to have to go through regular channels, not yet, if you know what I mean?"

He chuckled heartily. "You mean you need some under-the-radar cyber investigation done?"

"Yes."

His tone turned serious. "What is it that you need checked?"

"Background on a couple of companies. Got a pen?"

He grunted. "Fire away."

"The Nexus Research and Development Group, Science Reach International, and BioMed Pharmaceutical. I need to know who owns what, I mean behind-the-scenes, Harv, behind the shells and holding companies. I want to know whether they're ultimately U.S.-based, and if they are linked in any way." She paused. "And I want to know if there are any anomalies with the major shareholders, any unusual patterns, that kind of thing. How long will that take you?"

"That's real broad, Olivia. Could take a while, maybe a few days—"

"I don't have a few days, Harv. It's urgent."

He was silent for a while. "Are you okay? Is there something more I should know about?"

She blinked back the sudden burn in her eyes. "I…just need this done. Soon."

"Gotcha. I'll move it to the top of my agenda. Total priority."

Relief swooped through her. "I love you, Harv."

"I wish."

She tried to smile.

"Is there anything else?"

"Yes, there is. The FDS—Force du Sable. It's a private military company. I want to know exactly when it was founded, who founded it, who runs it, who the key players are, where the organization is registered, where they do their banking, and who hires them. Anything and everything. A photo of their main man would be good."

"That would be the PMC that's been lobbying the UN for some kind of international security commission."

"That's the one."

"Shouldn't be too tough to dig up stuff on them. They'd have had to put a lot of cards on their table to make their case for legitimacy. Anything else?"

"Not yet. Oh, wait, if you can find anything on a Dr. Paige Sterling and her work it would very much appreciated. I believe she's affiliated with an offshore lab in Hamān." She didn't want to give Harvey more. If the links were there, he would find them.

"Hamān? Where the uprising is—the one that's thrown the entire Middle East into chaos?"

"Yes, that Hamān."

Silence. "Olivia…if there's anything else you need, you call me, you understand? Any time of day or night. I don't know what you're into here, but…I'm behind you, okay?"

"Thanks, Harv." She hung up before emotion choked her throat. She tilted her head back, closed her eyes, tried to gather herself, and then she made another quick call, this one to her father's personal assistant. She asked him if her father would be in the office this morning. His assistant said he would. Olivia told her she'd be in to see him around 11 a.m.

She flipped her phone shut, brushed her teeth, fixed her hair and put on some makeup. Olivia studied her reflection, thinking. She looked vaguely normal and felt anything but.

As she turned to go, the glimmer of diamonds on the basin edge caught her attention. She stopped, stared at Grayson's ring, then quickly scooped it up and slipped it into her purse along with her phone.

Olivia walked softly over the carpet to the bedroom door, opened it just a crack and peeked through. The door to the study was closed. She listened. She could hear him in there, talking on the phone.

Her heart began to race. She tiptoed carefully over the wooden floor. Almost breathless with nerves, she opened her front door and fled from her own apartment.

Olivia stepped into the streets of Manhattan, heart thudding.

The light was bright and the air crisp. The storm clouds had cleared and the sky between the tops of buildings was eggshell blue. It all looked so normal— people rushing to work, going about their business, cars honking, taxis jostling.

She glanced over the road. The silver sedan was still there, but she couldn't see behind the tinted windows. She took a quick look to the left, then turned and walked down the street in the opposite direction, making for the subway that would take her south toward Venturion Tower in Manhattan's financial district.

She didn't see the motorbike that pulled out behind her and threaded innocuously into the traffic.

"She's on the move," the biker said into his head-piece. "She's asked someone at UN headquarters to dig into company structure, covertly. It's clearly someone she trusts. His name is Harvey. We've checked him out. He sometimes goes by the nickname Mobo— abbreviation for motherboard. He's some kind of tech-no-guy."

"We can't afford a leak now."

"It's okay, we're on it. We're moving into position to take him down as we speak."

"Hold off until he gives her the information she wants. It'll back our case. Take him right after."

"Affirmative. She also called Venturion. She's going to see Killinger at eleven. She's heading south. I'll keep a visual for as long as I can."

Jack pursed his lips. "Back off a little, McDonough. Give her the illusion of space. She needs it. We'll keep tabs via the GPS. I'll head her off at Venturion Tower before eleven."

He showered fast, cracked open the small tube he'd been carrying in a pouch in his coat lining, and ran the pitch-black dye quickly through his hair. He dried it using Olivia's dryer. He leaned forward over the basin and put in the dark-brown, almost-black contacts. He stood back, appraised himself in her bathroom mirror. The minor additions had changed his look in a major way. It was a simple but highly effective disguise, especially to someone who hadn't seen him in sixteen years—to someone who thought he was dead. Age, hard life, physical exercise, sun and wild weather in extreme environments had wrought the rest.

Jack knew he looked different—harder, older, meaner. He touched his scar with his fingertips, wondering if Olivia thought it looked grim. There was nothing nice about the way it pulled at the corner of his top lip, especially when he smiled. It was one of the reasons he never did.

It felt weird. Tight.

He picked up the empty tube of dye and caught sight of the slim gold chain hanging over the edge of the basin. It was broken. He picked it up, draped it through his fingers. The Saint Catherine's pendant spun, bouncing light and memories through his mind. He clenched his jaw and slipped the locket into his pocket, wondering what she'd done with the ring.

He walked through her room, the depth of the carpet pile absorbing his tread. He stopped, just to drink it all in—her clothes on the bed, her fragrance in the air, the elegant femininity of her decor. He closed his eyes for a moment, just letting the sensations flow over him, wondering if he would ever be in a room like this again, once this mission was over.

Then he left the apartment.

Olivia stopped at a coffee shop to summon her courage before she crossed the Venturion Tower Plaza and went up to meet her father on the top floor of his shimmering citadel high above most of Manhattan.

She ordered a latte, extra shot, and seated herself on a stool at the counter in front of the floor-to-ceiling windows that looked out over the plaza.

She cradled her coffee in her hands as she ran over potential scenarios in her mind for the zillionth time, a part of her waiting, putting it off.

Why?

Because she didn't want to know that the man who'd raised her since the death of her mother when she was five, could do something like this—to her, to Jack, to her country.

She didn't want to find out that he had intentionally killed innocent people in the Congo. She just could not fathom it. She trusted him. This was her *dad*—the guy who'd been there for her every step of the way after her mum was killed in a terrible car accident. Her dad had been driving that car—too fast. And although he chose never to speak about that fateful night to Olivia, she knew—*could see*—his feelings of guilt. And he'd done everything in his power to make her life smooth and beautiful because of it, in spite of it or simply because he loved her. It didn't matter. He'd been there for her. Always. *He* was the one who'd mended her scraped knees, who had waited outside for her on her first day of school. This was the man who'd left his office to come and help her shop for her prom dress, who'd waited up all night to ensure she got home safe.

He was the only parent she had.

Emotion swelled painfully in her chest. She fingered the silver cuff, maneuvering it around her wrist so that she could look at the pale-gold capsule under the small window of glass. She tried to yank if off again, and again, until she realized the woman next to her was watching with great curiosity.

Olivia shifted on her stool, away from the woman's line of sight, and rubbed her sore wrist. All she'd done was make it red. She was beginning to think it was a scam, that there was no GPS in this thing. No one had come chasing after her.

She sipped the last of her latte and plopped the cup in the garbage. Caffeine lifting her spirits, she ran lightly up the concrete steps, and made her way across the plaza. The sun was bright and leaves skittered crisply across her path with the cool breeze. Everything was going to be fine, she told herself. She was going to see her father and—

Her phone chimed.

Her heart kicked. She glanced around. There were two men wearing suits and dark glasses standing near the sculpture that dominated the plaza. There was something about their stance that didn't fit in, the way they didn't seem to be rushing anywhere. It made her nervous.

Her phone chimed again. She ferreted in her purse, found her cell, put it to her ear. "Hello?" She glanced over her shoulder. There was also someone standing at the base of the stairs. Was he watching her? Suddenly it seemed everyone in the plaza could be a spy, a tail. She was going totally paranoid.

"Hey, it's me, Harv."

Relief punched through her. Then tension reared right back up. "You got answers *already?*"

"Am I good or what?"

"Spill it, Harvey, quick."

"Okay, okay, the FDS was established ten years ago, by four men—Jacques Sauvage, Hunter McBride, Rafiq Zayed and December Ngomo. The force is about five hundred strong, and they hire freelance professionals when they need them. Sauvage is their lead man. I'm sending his mug to your cell as we speak. These guys have built a phenomenal rep in the last decade, Olivia. If you read between the lines, they've contracted to a covert arm of the CIA, among other high-profile organizations. Black-ops stuff. It's a lean force, but they're clean and they're heavy hitters." He paused. "You want to know something real funky?"

"Sure." She wasn't sure at all. Olivia glanced at the bench. She had a sense she was going to need to sit down.

"This Zayed guy, he's a bona fide Sultan. *He* is the missing heir to the Sultanate of Hamān—the guy who's causing all that mayhem in the Middle East right now. He's been hiding in the Legion, and then in the FDS under a new name for all these years. And now he's back to claim his throne."

Olivia was quiet. She seated herself on the bench. Cold nosed into her coat. The breeze ruffled her hair.

"You still there?"

"Go on."

"You already know this stuff, don't you, Olivia? You're onto something major here."

"I…I just needed some kind of third-party confirmation. And, Harvey, this…this is highly confidential, okay? I can't stress that enough."

He was silent for a while. When he spoke again, his voice was uncharacteristically serious. "I hear you, Olivia. But if you need help—"

"I will call, I promise. Did you get anything on Dr. Sterling?"

"Yeah, and I'm guessing this is not a coincidence, either. She was working for Nexus—one of the companies you asked me to look into."

"Was?"

"Yeah, she's deceased, apparently. She had a freak car accident. Her vehicle went clean over the cliff into the Red Sea a few days ago. She was one of their top scientists."

We brought her out of Hamān three days ago. She's working in a level-four lab we have set up on São Diogo.

"Did…did she have this accident around the time this Zayed guy appeared in Hamān?"

"Maybe two or three days before he hit the radar. You think there's a link?"

"Tell me about Nexus."

"Clandestine drug development and research company. The entire lab compound was burned to the ground, ostensibly by rebels during the coup. All records have vanished."

Olivia put her hand to her temple, pressed.

"Strange set of coincidences…or not."

She cleared her throat. "Harvey, is Nexus linked in any way to Science Reach International or BioMed?"

"Yep. Science Reach International apparently funds field research that is further developed in labs by the Nexus group. Science Reach underwrote a research project conducted on Bonobos—pygmy chimps—by Dr. Sterling's parents in the Congo. Curiously enough, they vanished in the jungle when their daughter was fifteen. It was a big mystery in the papers back then, still unsolved from what I can see. I'm not one hundred percent clear on the BioMed links yet, but so far it looks as if grant money for Science Reach research comes from the pharma corporation, and that Nexus drug patents are picked up by BioMed. I'll have to dig further to get anything definitive."

"How easy was it get this information?"

"The only reason I have this stuff is because you showed me where to look, provided me with the connections. Without that knowledge I'd probably still have zip. You want me to keep digging?"

Heaviness swamped her like a wet cloud. She glanced up at the shimmering tower of glass spearing into the sky. "No, not right now. I owe you big-time. I really do."

"You sure you don't want to talk about this, Olivia?"

"No, it's okay, thank you."

"Look, I'm going to give you my private cell number. Call me anytime, day or night, I'll answer."

She took it down, and then studied the digital photo Harvey had sent to her phone. Jacques—Jack—stared back at her, his Arctic eyes cool, his scar a stark warning to those who dare cross him. There was no question—it was him all right.

If Jack had done work for CIA, it was conceivable Elliot might have turned to him if all else failed him at home. A secret part of her was thrilled at the notion of her old lover leading an army, fighting for the underdog from the dark shadows of society; while at the very same time a tightness gripped her chest and strangled her throat at the notion her father was his target.

And she was smack in the middle.

Olivia closed her phone slowly, looked up. The city looked different. The air felt colder.

Dad, what have you done?

She shook herself. Nothing. He'd done nothing. He was innocent until proven guilty, just like everyone else. She thought of Jack…and felt gray. She hadn't done Jack that same small service all those years ago. She'd believed in his guilt because he'd run, because he hadn't stood up against the charges, because her father, his lawyers, the police and the evidence had all indicated he was guilty.

Suddenly she was sure of nothing.

All she knew was that Jack's information checked out with Harvey's. It appeared he was telling the truth on those counts. But it still just didn't make sense. A president didn't just stand down, unless he was sick or incapable of governing in some way. And what if Elliot did stand down, in spite of what Jack said? He would still be around. He could still talk about what he'd been forced to do.

Olivia pushed her windblown hair off her face. Was it because of this threat that Elliot had moved to exclude Grayson from his ticket? The official message was divergent policies, views on governing. How long had Elliot *really* known about this?

The more she thought about it, the more questions she had. Her phone rang again and her pace quickened.

She flipped it open, glanced around the plaza, put it to her ear. "Hello?"

"Olivia, it's Pria." There was fear in her voice

Nerves whipped through Olivia. "Pria, what is it?"

"I…I'm not sure. I just thought you should know."

"What?"

"There were two guys here…they came for Harvey. He was working on our floor. I saw him leave with them. They…took him."

Her eyes shot around the plaza. *"What* two guys, Pria? Where did they go?"

"I don't know! They came to your office first. I…got a bad feeling. I know he was just talking to you, and I thought you might want to know."

Nausea swooped through her. "Thanks, Pria. I…I'll be in touch. I'm going to try and reach him on his cell."

With shaking fingers she punched in Harvey's number. It rang. And rang. And rang.

Pick up, Harv.

No answer. No voice mail. Nothing.

Day or night, I'll answer.

Something was stopping him from answering.

They're heavy hitters.

Oh God, had she put him in trouble? Had Jack's men done this? She glanced wildly around. Who was watching, listening? Was her cell being monitored? She felt naked, exposed, way out of her depth. Frightened.

She stood, her knees weak. Her dad, she had to see her dad. She started to walk woodenly toward the revolving glass doors that opened like a mouth at the base of the glass tower. Her vision narrowed to a tunnel, and a buzz filled her head. She focused on getting to those doors.

But before she could reach them, movement blurred darkly to her left.

She gasped, started to run.

But a hand grabbed her shoulder, jerked her back. She opened her mouth to scream, but before sound could escape her throat, she was flung around and a mouth pressed down hard over hers.

Chapter 7

10:45 *Romeo. Venturion Plaza.*
Manhattan. Wednesday, October 8.

Shock weakened her knees, and Olivia felt her body sag. But he held her up, his hand firm at the small of her back, pulling her body hard up against his. He deepened his kiss and she knew the taste and feel of him instantly.

Jack.

"Don't fight," he murmured against her lips. "They're watching us." He moved his hand lower down her back, drew her into his coat, closer, pressing her breasts against the solidness of his chest. "You are my lover, Olivia," he whispered over her mouth, his breath warm, mingling with hers in the cold fall air. "That's how it must look to them."

She stilled in his arms, her heart kicking hard against her ribs. "Who…who is watching?" she whispered against his lips.

"Your father's men."

"Where?" Her words were coming out breathy.

"Behind me," he murmured over her mouth, "in front of the sculpture."

So she'd been right about them. Her heart began to palpitate.

"And over to our right, at the hotdog stand."

She felt trapped. She *was* trapped—in the iron grip of his loving arms, his big black coat swirling about them, the chill fall wind blowing her hair about their faces in an intimate curtain.

He pulled her closer, into the warmth of his big wool coat, nuzzled her neck, his stubble harsh against her skin, his breath soft against her ear, his scent enveloping her. Heat diffused through her stomach. "What are you doing, Jack?"

"My job," he whispered.

He caressed her hair, making like a lover, adoring her in public, and she felt her heart melt—not because of the sensuality in his caress, but because of the tenderness, the care, the sense of male proprietorship. Her eyes filled with emotion. No one had touched her like that since he left. Not with that kind of…love.

"And," he whispered under her hair, "may I remind you of the consequences of revealing my identity to your father."

The reality of their situation slapped back. He really was just doing his job, giving her a final warning before she went into that building and up that elevator. "You've made it quite clear, Jack," she said, trying to pull back.

But he held her tight. "Olivia—" The sound of gravel rolled through his French accent. "I want you to inform your father you are seeing someone other than Forbes and have been for some time, exclusively, in Europe, until now."

"Why?"

"It'll explain my sudden presence and our intimacy to those men watching us right now. It will enable us to move freely, together, as a couple," he whispered against her ear.

She swallowed. A couple? *Lovers,* he'd said earlier. The idea sent both fear and anticipation rippling through her. What would it be like, to feel him again inside her again, to feel so alive again?

His lips brushed her earlobe, twisting ribbons of tension through her stomach. "Your lover, Olivia, is Belgian. His name is Henri Devilliers. You met him through your UN work in Den Hague."

He moved his mouth along her cheek to the corner of her lips. "You've seen him on each of your European trips for the past three years. You think you love him. He's come to America on business and to visit you. You think it is time you tell your father about him. Your father's men have seen me in your apartment already. They are watching us now. The cover will fit."

The warmth of his voice sent molten fire spearing through her middle. "Kiss me now, Olivia, before you go up to see your father."

Her heart hammered against her chest. She turned her face to his, her lips finding his, and her brain spun into a maelstrom of sensations. He held back, waiting for her to make the moves, to accept the charade. But was it a charade? It didn't feel like a pretense—every molecule in her body was suddenly screaming for him to touch her, open her, love her. Like he used to. She feathered her lips softly over his, and his breathing became hard. It made her mind blank, her body suddenly wild inside. She ran her tongue over his lips, testing, tasting. They were firm, tasted of salt and a wild foreignness. She found the corner where his scar met his mouth, let her tongue explore, gently, softly, before parting his lips, and letting herself in.

A low, soft moan escaped his chest. He yanked her hard into himself, thrust his tongue deep, and Olivia felt herself explode into sensation deep in places she had long forgotten. She was coming alive, combusting into a thousand burning flames of sensation that screamed for more fuel.

She pulled back sharply, breathless, her skin pulsing with each beat of her heart. She looked up into his eyes—and her heart stalled.

She was looking into the face of a stranger. His arctic eyes were almost inky black. And so was his hair. It made his skin seem darker. It made him look exotic, dangerous.

If he had appeared at her door looking like that, after sixteen years, she would not have recognized him. She would have needed a great deal of convincing to believe that it was in fact the man she was once going to marry.

He slipped a pair of black shades over his eyes. "Ready?"

She glanced toward the doors of her father's building. And the choices she faced could not be more stark. Her future, her whole life, hung on the moves she would make now.

"Olivia?"

She nodded. "I'm ready."

He touched two fingers to her lips and blew her a kiss. "I'll be waiting. Right here."

She inhaled deeply, turned and headed for the revolving doors. Then she hesitated, stopped, turned back to face him.

Worry crossed his features.

"He'll check on you. He'll look Henri up."

"And he'll find that Henri exists." He came up to her, placed his hand on her arm, just above the bracelet. A subtle reminder? "It's okay, Olivia," he said. She couldn't see his eyes behind the black glasses. "If he looks, he will see that Henri Devilliers entered the States yesterday. He's an arms dealer, a shadowy character who will make him very nervous. He won't be happy that Henri is seeing his daughter. It will worry him, eat at him."

"You're trying to force his hand, aren't you?"

He pursed his lips, shrugged slightly, in a casual off-handed manner that made him seem incredibly European.

"How come he will find this Henri exists?"

"He's a ghost, a cipher of sorts we created some years ago to facilitate various weapons transactions. He's a convenient cover when we need him. And we've just added you to his portfolio of interests—or conquests, shall we say."

She studied him, wondering where Henri began and where Jacques ended, and how her old Jack really fitted inside this man. There was so much that was familiar about him, yet so much that was foreign, dangerous. Sinister. And exciting—if you were into high-risk adrenaline. And deadly secrets.

"Did you take Harvey, Jack?"

"Harvey is safe, Olivia. We can't afford loose ends right now."

So his men *had* taken him. It was her fault. She'd brought this on her friend. She glared at Jack. "If anything happens to him—"

"It won't."

A bubble of resentment erupted deep inside her. "So you're monitoring my cell phone."

He said nothing. Even his expression was silent.

She stared at him, trying to read him. She hated the idea of his men listening to her, just as much as she abhorred the notion of her father spying on her. The sooner she got to the bottom of this, the sooner she could get back to her old life. If she spent too long with Jack, she was going to get burned. That she knew already. The only thing she could do now was to try to control the degree.

She spun on her heels, took the last steps to the revolving door and entered the tower—committed now to going in, all the way to the truth. And its consequences.

The revolving door emptied her into the huge Venturion lobby, and she felt momentarily disoriented. The black expanse of marble floor gleamed around her. Fountains splashed into rectangular glass pools. The doormen, flanking the entrances like sentries, nodded politely to her. She hadn't really ever noticed how much they looked like bouncers as opposed to doormen. She looked up at the vaulted skylights, searching for cameras. She hadn't really given them much thought before, either, though she'd known they were everywhere.

Heart pumping, she crossed the marble floor and made for the row of bronze elevator doors.

Sun streamed through the wall-to-wall windows of her father's vast office, bouncing off chrome and glass and gleaming polished wood. The towers of Manhattan sparkled below.

Olivia inhaled deeply, flicked her hair back over her shoulders, clutched her purse tightly in front of her and entered the door.

"Olivia!" He got up from his desk immediately, came straight over to her, kissed her warmly on the cheek, then he went to close the door behind her.

"I'm so glad you came." He took her hands in his, instantly catching sight of the silver bracelet. A frown flickered over his brow. "Jewelry?"

Nerves scattered through her. "It's…a gift," she said, thinking about what the contents of that little gold capsule could do, of the Congo footage Jack had shown her, of those innocent villagers. Of her dad's alleged involvement.

He lifted her hand to examine the silver cuff. "It's unusual," he said, turning her wrist over.

"I know." She forced a smile. "It's a designer piece. Kind of artsy, don't you think?"

"You don't wear anything like this. You hardly ever wear jewelry at all."

Why was he pushing the issue? He'd never commented on her jewelry preferences before. Was he perhaps looking for the ring from Grayson, wondering why it wasn't on her finger?

"The giver was rather insistent that I wear it."

His smile faded and his eyes turned cool. "Who is he, Olivia?"

She withdrew her hands quickly, walked over to the windows, her heart racing a million miles per minute. She stared out at the cityscape, beautiful in the fall sunshine. But the beauty seemed somehow removed. "You knew there was someone in my apartment last night, didn't you, Dad?" She turned to face him. "That's why you phoned at that hour, wasn't it?"

A strange look shifted into his eyes. He said nothing.

"You're having me watched, aren't you?"

He didn't move a muscle in his face, and when he spoke, his words were carefully measured. "Why don't you sit, honey, let's talk."

"No, I'm okay standing, thanks. I want to know why you have men spying on me."

He sighed. "Don't put it like *that,* Olivia."

Her heart sunk. So it was true. Her own father, the man she had always trusted, had people spying on her, reporting back to him. She felt truly violated.

"I want to know why."

He didn't miss a beat. "You have no Secret Service protection, Olivia. Grayson is a powerful man, and that makes *you* a target, even if you don't want to accept it. I just want to know that you're safe, honey."

Those men probably have orders to get you out of the country ASAP if things go sideways....

He stepped forward, reached for her hands again. "You mean the world to me."

"I...I know, Dad." *That's why Jack is using me to get to you.* She felt sick—used. "But I want you to call those men off. It makes me feel...defiled. It's an invasion of my privacy. If you felt so strongly about this, the least you could have done was tell me."

"You'd have refused, Olivia."

"Yes, I would have." Olivia stared at him. "Will you call them off?"

"Of course, sweetheart."

"At once?"

"Anything you want."

Silence stretched awkwardly between them. Her heart began to thud again.

"What happened with Grayson?" he said finally.

She sighed. "I'm not going to marry him, Dad. I told him I needed time to think about it. I didn't want to break it off with him until he left office, but I'll have to now."

His jaw tensed. "Why?"

"Because...because I'm seeing someone else."

Shock flickered through his eyes and then was gone. "Who is he, Olivia?" His tone was devoid of emotion. "Was he the man in your apartment last night?"

"His name is Henri Devilliers. He's Belgian. I met him in Den Hague. He's here on business and he's come to see me." The lie came out too easily. And she despised herself for it.

The muscles in her father's neck bunched tight, but his voice remained level. "How long have you been seeing him?"

"A few years." Another lie, another little step toward deceit, betrayal. But he had also betrayed her trust by having her watched without telling her. It made her feel ill. It was *not* a father's right.

He exhaled sharply, ran his hand over his blond hair. "This is a bit of a...surprise, Olivia. When were you going to tell me."

"I...I was going to tell you this week, while Henri was in town, but you forced my hand by having me followed."

"How serious are you, with this...this man?" His voice had taken on an edge. That was unusual—and a measure of just how much she'd upset him. Her father was usually a model of self-control.

"I think I love him."

He paled, turned his head away sharply, then whipped it back. He wasn't hiding his anger at all now. It was glittering in his eyes.

"Olivia, you should have told us this."

"Us?"

He hesitated. "Me, and Grayson of course, he *deserves* to know."

The strands of doubt Jack had planted in her mind threaded closer, weaving together in a soft web.

"My personal business with Grayson is just that, Dad. Mine. Personal." And inside she knew a part of herself was pushing, fishing. She needed to see just how connected her father and Grayson were behind her back.

He ran his hand over his hair again, another sign of his distress. "Look, I'm sorry, Olivia. I'm just worried about…things at the moment. And you *know* I'd love to see the two of you together. You make the perfect, beautiful couple." He smiled warmly, and his eyes were light again. "Forgive me. Why don't you stay for a while? I can have some lunch brought up. We can talk about this."

She shook her head, feeling a sudden overwhelming loss. "I…Henri and I have plans."

He nodded slowly. "All right. But be careful, Olivia."

"Careful?"

"You don't really know this man—"

"I know him very well, Dad."

He grinned. "I guess I mean *I* don't know him. It's a father thing. When will I get to meet him?"

She swallowed against the pinch of tension in her throat. "Soon. I…I'll speak to him, ask him."

He nodded, something hidden in his eyes. "Well, I'll be seeing you on Monday, then."

"Monday?" she said, momentarily confused.

"The thirteenth," he reminded her. "The yacht, the big announcement, remember?"

Her heart kicked sharply against her ribs. "Of course. You…you never mentioned what the announcement was going to be."

He smiled. "It's a surprise. I don't want to tip off our stockholders prematurely."

"Of course," she said again, her voice strangely flat to her own ears. "Unfortunately, I don't think I can make it, Dad. I plan to be in Los Angeles with Henri on that date. He has some business there."

The words just came out of her mouth. She just needed to say them. She wanted to give him a chance to prove it was all a lie—that there were no bombs set to detonate in Los Angeles, Chicago or New York. She desperately wanted to hear that he had no objection to her going to L.A. on that date.

But his hands tensed at his side and a small vein popped out on his temple. "I need you with me, Olivia," he said quietly. He stepped up to her. "I need you there in your mother's place. Do this for me, please. It's a major coup for Venturion, for me, for *all* of us." He took her hands. "She'd want you there, by my side."

She stared at him in shock. How dare he? How dare he throw her mother into this, play on those emotions in her. She sucked in a deep breath. "I'm sorry, Dad. I'm sure you'll all do just fine without me." She walked past him, aimimg for the door, feeling like something had been stolen from her, feeling more alone and lost than she could ever remember.

Samuel Killinger felt his heart break as he watched his daughter leave. She was slipping from his grasp, his control. He could feel it.

He stalked over to the windows, rammed his hands into his pockets and glared at the skyline. She looked so much like her mother. She *was* so much like her mother. She was the living, breathing symbol of the love he and his wife had shared…before the crash.

Before he'd killed his wife by driving too fast, before

his love of speed and impossibly expensive cars had stolen the woman he loved above all—Genevieve. His childhood sweetheart. His beautiful young bride. The only woman he had truly ever wanted in his bed. The only woman who had made him feel completely whole.

Yet *he* was the one who had destroyed her.

Bitterness, guilt and self-hatred seethed through him. He'd never been able to stanch the cesspool of destructive emotions that haunted him over that fateful night. He'd never managed to dull the raw pain when he thought of her.

He didn't even want to. Holding on to the pain kept his love alive.

And so did Olivia.

Olivia represented everything that was good and true and beautiful in his life, and Samuel wanted nothing but the best for her. He wanted to keep her *safe*. From destructive men like himself. From men like Henri Devilliers. Who in hell was he anyway?

Anger pulsed at his temples.

Where had he come from? *Why now?* This was a really rotten time for his daughter to go searching for whatever it was she felt was lacking in her life. And what in hell was wrong with Forbes that he couldn't hold on to a woman? Forbes had looks, wealth, power…and soon he'd be one of the most powerful men in the world.

He spun around, grabbed the phone on his desk, jabbed a button. "Keep watching her," he said sharply. "But be extremely careful. She's made you. I do *not* want her to see you again. And I want everything you can dig up on that man she's with—and I mean *everything*. His name is Henri Devilliers. I want to know where he was born, who his parents are, where he went to school, what he does for a living. I want to know what he eats for breakfast, lunch and dinner. I want to know which way he brushes his goddamn teeth! I want to know about every woman he's ever screwed in his entire life! Got it?"

He hung up, his blood pressure soaring. This was not good. He *never* lost it with his men.

He sucked air deep into his lungs, blew it out in a controlled stream, then picked up the phone again. "Vice President Forbes, please. It's Samuel Killinger. It's urgent."

When Forbes came on the line, Killinger wasted no time on pleasantries.

"Olivia is seeing another man."

Silence stretched over the distance to Washington.

"Who?" The single word hummed with quiet, dark fury.

"His name is Henri Devilliers. We're running a check on him as we speak. Apparently, she's been seeing him for several years—in Europe, which is why we never picked up on it. We should have put that tail on her earlier."

"How could you have allowed this to happen?" said Forbes.

Killinger felt himself begin to vibrate with anger all over again, but he kept his voice level. "I should be asking *you* that question, Grayson. The man clearly possesses something you don't." *Like balls.*

"I don't like the timing. I want *everything* on this man," Forbes snapped.

"Like I said, we're on it." Killinger hung up quietly, trying to control his anger at Grayson Forbes. He could give the man a presidency, but he could not give him mojo.

He stalked back to the window, his mind racing. If Olivia refused to come to his yacht, he would have to find another a way to get her out of the country—before Monday.

Chapter 8

11:59 Romeo, Venturion Plaza,
Wednesday, October 8.

Jack was outside, waiting, pacing the plaza, his big black coat moving like a cape behind him.

He stilled the instant he saw her.

Olivia glanced around nervously. The men she'd seen earlier were gone. People seemed to be walking with purpose, no one looking at her. Had her father called the bodyguards off already? His power was suddenly frightening. She knew he wielded influence, but she'd never been on the receiving end. It had never scared her before.

The seeds of doubt planted by Jack were taking root in her soul. As was a growing sense of loss.

She began to walk away from him, unable to face him. She was mourning inside, grieving the bond she thought she'd had with her father.

Olivia was only beginning to understand how potent an influence her father may have been in her life behind the scenes, how blind she might have been to his machinations.

She could see Jack in her peripheral vision. He was coming after her, cutting across the plaza with smooth, confident movements. Her heart quickened. She was afraid of him, too—of his intensity, of her own reawakened desire for him.

He caught up to her, grabbed her, whirled her round and kissed her as if he owned her.

He *did* own her. For now anyway. She was bound to him by more than the metal cuff—she was committed to this journey to the bitter end. And whether she liked it or not, he was the one calling the shots.

He gripped her by the shoulders, held her at arm's length, his gaze piercing. "How did it go?"

He was uneasy. He'd handed her the equivalent of a loaded gun and had sent her up there trusting she wouldn't use it. Now he was worried she had.

"What happened, Olivia?"

She didn't want to talk about it. She didn't want her father to be guilty of anything. She wanted to believe in Jack. But that meant accepting too many other things. Oh God, she was going to throw up. "I just want to get out of here, Jack, please."

He removed his shades and studied her. The compassion and concern in his rough and arrogant features tugged at her, bringing tears threateningly close to the surface.

He nodded slowly. "*D'accord,*" he said, brushing her cheek gently with the backs of his fingers. "Where would you like to go?"

Her eyes began to burn and the world blurred. "The ocean. I'd like to go to the ocean, Jack. To the Hamptons." Where the wind would blow cold off the sea and clear her soul. Where she could think.

He looked pensive for a moment, then he bent down and kissed her cheek, like the lover he was pretending to be. But she didn't want to pretend.

She wanted him back.

She wanted to feel him inside, desperately, fiercely. She wanted to stand in public, right here in the middle of Manhattan, and kiss the man she'd once loved so passionately. Claim him back, erase the lost years, bridge this horrible chasm that yawned between them.

But that would mean *accepting* the past.

And she couldn't do that. She was still incapable of making that leap of faith, of admitting her life had been a total lie.

He stroked her hair, and she leaned instinctively into him, petrified that she was allowing herself to fall right into that gaping chasm.

But as he gathered her against his body, she felt protected. Safe. She cursed softly. Olivia hadn't had this need for a man in sixteen years. She'd forgotten how damn good it felt to just let go for an instant and lean on someone. She breathed deeply, inhaling the faint scent of tobacco.

"You don't smoke," she murmured into his lapel, not caring right now whether he did or didn't.

"Henri does."

She glanced up, met his eyes. Even with the dark contact lenses, he was suddenly the Jack she remembered. She'd missed him. So much.

He took a packet of cigarettes out of his coat pocket held them out for her to see. "Black tobacco," he said.

"Very European," she said.

"So is smoking. It's been an essential part of Henri's cover for years. Gives him a reason to lurk outside buildings."

She wondered how many times in his life he'd role-played like this. How much was fake right now?

"Don't worry," he said, misreading her consternation, "I don't inhale."

She huffed lightly. "They all say that."

The hint of a smile tugged at the corner of his mouth that met with the scar.

She reached up, touched the scar with her fingertips. He tensed slightly.

"You don't smile, do you, Jack? You used to."

She felt him pull away, distance himself. He lifted his shoulder in a shrug. "It pulls at the scar, feels weird." And he was closed again, his voice hard again, the old Jack gone again. "Come, I have a car waiting. You can tell me about your meeting on the way."

"On the way to where?"

"The Hamptons, of course. We'll go pick up your things first."

Back to the ocean. The past.

He took her arm, escorted her across the plaza, his eyes and movements watchful.

"They're gone," she said following his gaze. "The men, I told him I didn't want them, and they're gone."

"No, they're still there."

"I don't see them."

"That's because they don't want you to."

"I asked him to take them off."

"Olivia, this is your life we're talking about. He's not going to gamble with that. He's going to want those men and that antidote close to you at all times. Don't look now, but across the road, under the row of trees, there's one there. And there's another behind us, near the stairs."

She stole a quick glance, couldn't help it. And she saw the man across the road.

Her father had lied to her—again.

Jack led her up to a sports car, a low white convertible with the top down. Olivia noted the badge on the hood—a Lamborghini.

"This is yours?"

"Henri's. He's got a thing for foreign sports cars, especially the Italian ones," he said with a wink as he opened the passenger door for her. "The rental company couldn't accommodate my request for the special edition, which, of course, Henri would have preferred. But the Gallardo Spyder does have some nice features—like the retractable roof, the four-wheel drive and the video camera on the rear spoiler."

He closed her door, climbed in the driver's side, angled his head. "Got to keep up appearances, you know?"

She shook her head, amused. He truly was gorgeous. He meshed his rugged power with an urban sensibility in a way her father and Grayson never could. He made her stomach swoop. He made her warm in places she shouldn't be thinking about right now. Her gaze fastened involuntarily on his lips, and her mind began to wander.

"What are looking at?"

"I…I'm just wondering how many women Henri has back in Europe." How many mouths those lips have kissed. And she heard the soft husky tone in her own voice.

He stilled, his eyes holding hers. Something subtle shifted in his features and the energy in the cockpit was suddenly tangible, dark.

Then he snorted, severed the contact and started the car. The Lamborghini roared to life and purred throatily, causing the car to vibrate gently under her.

"Because if my father finds out you have a whole bunch of ladies tucked away in Europe somewhere—"

"Ah, so you *did* tell him about Henri?" She heard the relief in his voice.

She nodded.

"How'd he take it?"

"Not well."

"You tell Forbes?"

"Not yet."

He shifted into first gear. "He probably knows by now, anyway." And he swerved into the traffic with an ostentatious, exhibitionist shriek of rubber on tar.

She braced her hand against the dash. "I suppose this

is how Henri drives?" she yelled into the wind over the snarl of the engine.

"Henri has speed issues." He hit the gas and swerved between cars, his eyes glancing up to the mirror.

"And what does *Jack* drive when he's at home?" she called into the wind as she tried to hold her hair down.

"Jack doesn't have a home, Olivia." He swerved in front of a cab, and the driver laid on the horn. She winced as tires screeched behind them.

"What about Jacques?" she yelled into the wind. "Does he have one?"

He accelerated suddenly, swerved, and she was flung sideways against the door.

She'd hit a sore spot, and he was taking it out on the road.

Olivia sat tense as a coiled spring, heart racing, fingers clutching the armrest, her hair whipping about her face as he snaked through the traffic at a maniacal speed. Maybe it was better if she died like this. Now. Then maybe she wouldn't have to face the road that lay ahead.

Tires screeched.

She squeezed her eyes shut, braced for the crunch of metal. But nothing came, just a sharp lurch to a stop and the throaty drone of the engine straining against the brakes. She peeked through her lids. He'd actually stopped for the red light, thank God.

She stole a quick glance at his profile. His hands rested loosely on the wheel in spite of the way he was commanding the car. He was a chameleon, shifting between personas as easily as he shifted the gears.

"I don't think it's Henri who has the speed issues," she said a little angrily. "Could you possibly drive just a bit slower?"

He glanced at her, but she couldn't read his eyes behind those black shades. The light turned green and he took off, at a quieter speed this time, slowing to an almost regular pace. She allowed the air in her lungs to escape. Had he just been trying to rattle her?

"Tell me what happened with your father, Olivia."

"I told him I was not going to marry Grayson. I told him I loved another man and that I was going to Los Angeles with him in six days."

His eyes shot to her.

"Watch out, Jack!"

He swerved easily, still looking at her.

"How the *hell* did you see that, you weren't even watching! Please, Jack, watch the road."

Silence.

She drew in a deep shaky breath.

"Why did you tell him that?"

"I don't know," she snapped, tension making her curt. "It just came out. I think I wanted him to prove to me that it wasn't an issue. I wanted him to prove that he didn't care where I was on the thirteenth."

"And he didn't."

"No, Jack, he didn't. He wants me out of the country on Monday. You happy now?"

They were forced to a stop by another traffic light, and he used the moment to cover her hand with his, give it a quick squeeze. "Good job, Livie."

"*Good?* At what? Deceiving my father?"

"I know it's tough, but you did great. You've forced his hand. He's going to try and find a way to get you out of the country now, and we'll be ready. It's more than we could have hoped for."

She didn't feel great about that at all. She closed her eyes, rested her head back into the neat little space designed for a head, nothing more.

"What was the plan before, Olivia? Where did he want you to be on the thirteenth?"

Her jaw tightened. Telling him would be handing him her father on a platter. She felt torn.

Then she thought of Harvey, of how she'd landed him in hot water. And she thought of the men still following her, in spite of her father's promise. Squeezing her eyes shut she saw flashes of those horrific images from the Congo.

She thought of the president, and how the nation loved him—and gave in.

"He wants me on his yacht in the Caribbean. The entire Venturion board will be there for some big announcement that night, along with their spouses and other high-powered guests." There, she'd done it. She'd just handed her dad to Jack and his mercenaries—but if her father *was* innocent, it wouldn't matter. It *shouldn't* matter.

Jack reached instantly for his phone. He pushed a button, put the phone to his ear, maneuvering just as deftly through traffic with one hand.

"McDonough, we have a location. The entire Cabal will be on a yacht—" he turned to her "—where in the Caribbean?"

Nerves skittered through her belly. It shouldn't matter, she reminded herself. "Off Little Cayman," she said. "Most of the guests will be transported from the big island."

"—Cayman Islands area. Get in touch with Mc-Bride. Start setting things up for a takedown at sea. We'll need divers, underwater surveillance equipment, boats—" he swerved sharply "—a vessel that looks like one of the fishing charters would be good. Pull our team out of Honduras. They're the closest, and we can spare them for a week or so. We'll need to be in position before Cabal members start arriving." He turned to her. "When will your father be there?"

She hesitated. He was making it seem so real. "He's supposed to be on his boat by the morning of the twelfth. It's called the *Genevieve*…after my mother."

He relayed the name to his man, and hung up. "You have *got* to get me on that yacht, Olivia."

"How in heaven am I supposed to do that, Jack? I just told my father I wasn't coming, that I was going with you to Los Angeles."

He turned into her street, slowed the vehicle as he approached her building. "He's not going to let that happen, believe me."

"And how do you think he is going to stop me?"

"Maybe he won't have to. Not if you tell him you're coming to the Caymans—*with* your date." He pulled to a stop outside her building. The doorman was already moving toward them, attracted by the car and the promise of a healthy tip. Jack cupped her cheek. "Thank you, Olivia, for trusting me."

"I don't." She looked away. "I don't trust you any more than I trust my own father right now."

"Why?" he said softly.

"*Why?* What kind of question is that?" she said, searching for a way to open the fancy door. The doorman beat her to it, opened it from the outside. She climbed out, waved her hand over the convertible. "Because none of this is real—this car, you, me, *us,* that's why. It's a charade. What's there to trust?"

Jack glanced pointedly at the doorman, warning her to tone it down. She shut her mouth, stormed into the building.

He caught up to her at the elevators, leaned his arm against the wall, trapping her. He brought his face close to hers. "Hang in there, Olivia," he said softly. "I know this isn't easy."

"Easy?" She huffed. "Easy doesn't even…come close…" Her voice trailed off. His mouth was so near. She could feel his breath warm over her lips. She could sense his energy. It literally pulsed through her, like it always had. This man was so alive. So vital. She swallowed, tried to look away, but he snagged her chin with his finger, forced her to look back into those dark glasses where all she could see was her own distorted reflection.

"Please, Livie."

Hot tears filled her eyes. She wanted him. She wanted Jack back. She wanted to tear those dark shades off his face, to see *him,* to know what was going on deep in his mind, at his core. She clenched her jaw in frustration as a tear slid down her cheek. He smoothed it away with the pad of his thumb and lowered his head.

"God, you have no idea how much I've missed you, Livie." His voice was thick and rough and it curled through her. He brushed his lips softly over her wet lashes.

Her throat tightened, and warmth pooled deep in her belly. The elevator bell clanged as the doors opened, and Olivia jumped, startled. She tried to regain her breath as they entered together. The doors slid shut, and it was just the two of them, cocooned and reflected many times over in smoky mirrors. The tension in the air was tangible. Hot.

Jack removed his glasses, and once again she was thrown by his black contacts, how darkly foreign he looked.

"I don't like pretending, Jack." She jabbed the button for her floor. "I don't like this charade."

He moved close to her. The elevator lifted, began to hum. "We don't have to pretend, Livie." His voice was low.

She tried to swallow. She could see her reflection in the mirrors, and she could see the flush of arousal on her own cheeks. It made her feel even hotter, more flustered, more aware of her sexual response to his presence.

He lifted his hand and trailed the backs of his fingertips up the side of her face, leaving a wake of exposed nerves.

"Jack." Her voice came out hoarse. "No one's watching now. You can cut the games."

He leaned forward, whispered against her ear. "You *know* this is no charade, Livie." His hand followed the line of her shoulder and trailed down the outside of her arm as he spoke. "Where in the Hamptons would you like to go?"

"I...I have a place on the beach," she managed to say.

His hand found her hip, and he splayed his fingers over it, moving gently around her rear. "So...a little trip back in time?"

She forgot how to breathe. She remembered the way they'd made love on the beach, in the sea, in front of the fire. Her throat grew thick, her brain fuzzy.

"Is it your place or your father's, Livie?" he whispered.

"It's...mine," she managed to say as he gripped her butt and pulled her hard up against him.

That was no charade pressing long and rigid against her pelvis. That was hard reality. That was him wanting her in the most basic way possible.

Her eyelids dipped and her vision blurred. "I... thought I told you not to call me that."

His hands explored the curves of her butt. "If you can call me Jack," he whispered hotly into her neck "I can call you Livie." He moved his hand around to the front of her thigh, and she began to ache for him to move his hand closer. She suddenly, desperately needed his touch at her throbbing, hot core. She arched her back, tilting her pelvis into his touch, giving him access, letting him know she wanted it, needed to feel him touch her.

His breathing became heavy, fast. He put his mouth over hers, parted her lips, thrust his tongue deep and cupped her hard between the legs. Olivia's knees went weak. She could feel the heat of his palm right through her clothes. Molten fire speared to her core. She moved against him, urgent, hungry, opening to him, needing him. He deepened his kiss, thrusting his tongue, moving the heel of his hand against her while his other hand reached for the wall, and he slammed the emergency stop button with his palm.

The elevator jerked and bounced to a sudden halt.

Somewhere in the back of her brain Olivia could hear a distant alarm bell begin to clang and she wondered if someone might see them on the security camera. But she couldn't stop, couldn't think. She was alive, aching, burning, like she hadn't burned in years. She was consumed with the need to feel his body against hers. She yanked his shirt out of his pants, desperately tore at the buttons, her hands seeking his skin, feeling him. He was warm, hard and muscled like rock, the hair of his chest rough under her fingers.

She could feel herself on the brink as his hand moved between her legs, coaxing her further. Her breaths became short and light. She felt dizzy. The elevator alarm was still clanging. They didn't have much time before someone would call for help. She reached for his belt, fumbled with the buckle, unzipped his pants, felt him swell hard and hot in her hands. A small groan of pleasure escaped her throat.

He reached round, undid the small zipper at the back of her pants, loosened them, slid them down her hips, sighed with hot pleasure as he discovered her G-string. He slid his hands along her buttocks, kneading her skin, her curves, parting her. He began to breathe harder, urgent, desperate.

She could hear banging on the elevator doors on one of the higher floors. "Hurry, Jack," she panted, "please…hurry."

He spun her around so that she faced the mirror. He moved her G-string aside, slid his hand between her legs, found her soft folds, slid his fingers up into her, slipped into her slick heat. He groaned, grabbed her breasts with one hand, parted her with his finger, and she felt him enter from behind, thick, hot. He thrust hard, deep. Olivia gasped, splayed her hands on the mirrors.

He thrust again and again, deeper each time, emotionally penetrating a part of her that had remained closed for years. Her hands steamed the glass, slid as she braced against his thrusts, her breaths escaping her in rhythmic exhalations.

She could see his face in the mirror. She watched his eyes, and he watched hers as he moved into her, stroking harder, faster, hotter. She dipped her back, moving her body against him, and suddenly she stopped, her mouth open, her pupils dilating until she could barely see…and she exploded with a sharp cry, her muscles contracting in powerful, rippling waves of release.

He grasped her hips with both hands, pumped hard, fast and climaxed with a deep guttural groan of pleasure.

She vaguely registered yelling upstairs, the alarm clanging, more banging on elevator doors.

She looked at him and smiled, then began to laugh lightly, then with release, abandon. She hadn't felt this good, had this much *fun* in…sixteen years.

He was watching her, intensely. Then the corner of

his lip twitched up into a lopsided grin, light dancing wickedly in his eyes. And it was the sexiest, most gorgeous thing she'd ever seen.

She leaned back against the mirror, steamy, her pants still loose around her hips, her silk shirt open, exposing a breast, her hair a wild mess. And she felt free, she felt whole, a woman—desirable and unfettered.

He arched a brow. "Do you know how truly beautiful you are?" he asked as he zipped up his pants. He reached for her blouse buttons, started doing them up for her as the banging and yelling upstairs increased. Olivia zipped her pants up behind her as he worked on her buttons. "I think our time is up," he whispered in her ear, and he gave her a quick kiss before he punched the release button.

The elevator began to rise. Olivia tried to smooth down her hair, and by the time the bell clanged for her floor, she'd pulled herself together. Sort of.

He slid his shades back over his eyes, took her hand in his. "Showtime," he whispered.

The doors opened to expose the very worried faces of Mr. and Mrs. Makarewicz, her neighbors from across the hall.

"Oh, goodness, Olivia, are you all right dear?"

She tried to keep her face serious, tried not to laugh at Jack's austere, haughty expression, the way he lengthened his spine and squared his shoulders.

"I'm fine, thank you."

"Was it stuck?" They were both looking at Jack with great curiosity.

"Not at all. Quite slick, actually," he said with a British accent as he led Olivia out by the hand and down the hall.

She could feel Mr. and Mrs. Makarewicz watching as they walked down the hall. "You're *evil*," she whispered.

He squeezed her hand tight. "I know. And you're damned hot," he said. "I'll ride an elevator with you anytime."

14:01 Romeo. Venturion Tower.
Wednesday, October 8.

"He's a *what!*" Killinger couldn't believe what he was hearing.

"An arms dealer, both black market and aboveboard. Runs a tight, secretive outfit, has extravagant taste—especially for fast cars and women. He's a Belgian national, born in Italy—Italian mother, Russian father. He was schooled around the world. Attended the Sorbonne. Very wealthy family, Russian mob connections. There's a period in his life where he seems to have dropped off the radar for a while. Not much on him for that time. He arrived in the States yesterday."

Killinger swore. What in hell had his daughter picked up? "He's traveling alone?"

"Can't be certain. He generally moves with close protection personnel, so they're probably around. We haven't seen them yet. People who cross swords with this guy tend to disappear or meet with unfortunate accidents."

Killinger cursed again. He'd bet his life Olivia didn't know what her new lover did for a living. It went against everything his daughter stood for.

"Henri Devilliers has made several trips to Den

Hague in the past three years that coincide with Olivia's. That's all we've manage to dig up on him so far."

"You still have a tail on them?"

"Yes. He's at her apartment. Gave us a bit of a ride through traffic. He's rented a Lamborghini, and he's using it."

Killinger thought of how his wife died. Fast cars and the men who used them were dangerous—he knew from personal experience. He hung up, and cursed violently. This was not the kind of man he wanted anywhere near his daughter. He checked his watch, picked up his phone again.

"Put the plan in action. I want her out of the country within the next twenty-four hours. Hold her until the deadline has passed."

"And Devilliers?"

"Kill him."

Chapter 9

14:59 Romeo. Olivia Killinger's apartment.
Manhattan. Wednesday, October 8.

Olivia left Jack talking quietly on his phone in the living room. She went into her bedroom, showered, dressed in jeans and a T-shirt and began packing an overnight bag. She was folding a shirt when she felt his presence.

She glanced up.

He was leaning against the doorjamb, taking her in lazily. That dark, sensual energy began to pulse between them again, and Olivia became acutely aware they were in her bedroom, that her bed was between them, that her underwear was spread out, waiting to be packed. Her eyes connected with his, and she knew they would make love again. Soon.

She knew in her heart she would sleep with him as often as she could—whenever, wherever she could. There was a sense of urgency, of the deadline looming. And she didn't know when she'd ever be with him again after that day.

She had no idea how much he really cared or how much he was manipulating her emotions and her body to get to his target. He was a mercenary, she reminded herself. And having sex was probably more pleasant than shooting someone—but it was still a means to an end.

She cleared her throat. "How long will we be gone?"

The look in his eyes grew darker, more intense, the energy between them edgier.

"Jack?"

"What did you do with his ring, Olivia?"

Surprise rippled through her. "I…it's in my bag. I…I have to give it back to him."

He nodded slowly. "Pack light, there's not much space in the Lamborghini. We can always pick up extra stuff if we need it."

She folded a pair of jeans. "What about you?"

"My guys will have some things in the car by the time we leave."

She zipped up her bag, stood up straight. "How many guys have you got out there, Jack?"

"Two outside. A few more in Manhattan. I'm mobilizing as many men as we can." He paused. "It would be good to have you on our team, Olivia. We could use your legal expertise."

"What do you mean?"

He stepped into her bedroom, and it shrank around

him. She thought of sex again, becoming conscious of the heat in her belly, the tenderness between her legs where he'd thrust into her. She could see in his eyes that he was thinking about it, too.

"You could help us push for an international commission to regulate the industry." He came close, touched her face. "You could work with us, Olivia. On São Diogo."

She blinked. She hadn't seen this coming. "I…I have a job, Jack."

He nodded, turned on his heels suddenly and left the room, sucking the energy after him like a vacuum. Confusion churned through her. "Jack!"

He stopped just outside the door.

"This…this army of yours, it's your way of hitting back at the world, isn't it? It's your way of striking back at my dad." She hadn't planned to say that. She didn't know what she'd intended to say. She just had a desperate need to engage him. She wanted to *know* him, understand the man he had become, and where she really stood in his life.

He turned slowly to face her. "No, Olivia. It's my way of doing what I believe in." He paused. "It's what *we* used to believe in, remember? Providing tools, resources, for the smaller guy to fight injustice." He stepped back into her room. "Same game, different name, Olivia. You do still believe, don't you?"

She sank on to the bed and buried her face in her hands, tired, drained, emotionally confused.

He came up to her, touched her hair. "You know in your heart your father is guilty, Olivia, even if your brain won't let you believe it." He picked up her bag.

"And you know in your heart that I am telling you the truth. I can see it in your eyes. Come," he said softly, "before it gets too late."

Olivia got up, sucked in a deep breath and took one last look around her apartment. She had a foreboding—a sense that she wasn't going to see it again. Or maybe she just wasn't going to be able to look at anything about her old life in the same way again. She'd crossed some kind of threshold, and there was no going back.

Was this the beginning of the end for them all?

15:02 Romeo. Central Broadcasting News Network. Washington. Wednesday, October 8.

"Something's off. Look—" The CBNN producer pointed to another clip. "Ruger is standing right beside Elliot in every shot. And there—freeze that frame, magnify it. See Ruger's face? He's looking really worried about something, and he's not leaving the president's side."

The producer popped another piece of nicotine gum into his mouth, chewed as he studied the frozen image of Dr. Sebastian Ruger. "If *that* man is worried," he said, "the nation should be worried."

He turned to his White House correspondent. "What do you think is going on?"

"Well, Elliot is lacking his usual energy. He seems…absent, unfocused—definitely out of character, he's sick."

"I think you're right."

"Do we say that?"

The producer pursed his lips. "No. We need more. For all we know he just has the flu. Speak to your White House contacts. But put some pressure on, tell them we know something's going on with the commander in chief's health, see what plays out."

"Why don't we just run with our speculation, hint at the fact he seems tired."

"Why?"

"Public deserves to know."

The producer shook his head. "No, our viewers deserve the truth, not rumor. Get on it, get me something I can use. We're on air again in—" he checked his watch "—less than four hours."

He cracked open a soda as the reporter headed back to his desk, then turned his attention back to the clip. He'd been covering presidents and elections for the past thirty years and he'd developed a gut sense for these things.

Something big was going down.

15:15 Romeo. New York.
Wednesday. October 8.

Jack drove fast into the early evening, clouds skudding high above them in an otherwise clear sky, the fall breeze refreshing, the top of the convertible still down. Olivia had tied a scarf around her hair and wore tinted shades to protect her eyes. Jack's men had put blankets and a basket of food and wine in the back. They'd even provided a collection of CDs—Italian opera, which Jack had blaring from the Lamborghini speakers as he drove. "What kind of merc are you anyway?" she said.

"Luxury model."

She smiled. "The Jack I used to know—this wasn't his style."

He glanced sideways at her, the hint of a smile tugging crookedly at his lips. "Ah, but my dear, this is the music and the life Henri would choose." He said it in a strong French accent. "And we are absolutely obligated to stay in character."

She studied his stark and handsome profile, his scar a reminder of his violent and ruthless streak. "You know, I have a sneaking suspicion that you enjoy playing the character of Henri Devilliers."

He threw back his head and laughed, and the sound made her feel light.

It was twilight by the time they neared the shore. The traffic had thinned and she could smell salt on the wind. Jack floored the gas pedal as they hit the coast road, and the wind tore her scarf loose from her hair. She caught it, lifted her chin, closed her eyes and let the briny breeze rush through her hair. Far from the city, she began to feel relaxed—free.

Jack turned up the music, and she let it wash over her. The smooth purr of the engine grew louder and louder as he increased speed, experimenting with the responsive handling of the sports car.

He turned a corner so fast it should have killed them, but the vehicle held. Olivia caught her breath, and a thrill rippled through her. She felt as if she were an outlaw, on the lam with Jack, her long-lost lover returned from the shadows. And whoever was trying to follow them now would be choking on their dust.

* * *

Jack stole a glance at Olivia. She was smiling to herself, her eyes closed, her hair swirling and bouncing about her face in the eddies of wind. She looked blissfully happy. Something soared wildly in his chest, and a new energy bit fiercely at him.

Not only did he want Killinger, now he wanted his daughter, as well. Completely. Forever.

She began to laugh beside him.

"What's so funny?" he asked.

She opened her eyes and even behind the tinted shades they glittered with light. "Nothing," she said with a smirk on her lips.

He nodded. "Ah, you're laughing at Henri, aren't you?"

"No," she said lifting her glasses and wiping her eyes. "I'm laughing at the whole damn world."

He frowned.

"Don't you see, Jack?" She leaned forward. "It's funny! Picture us—racing along in this crazily expensive car, my father's guys madly racing to catch up with us, your guys chasing after them, and where are we all going, really? To the beach? For a picnic? A trip back in time?" She sat back again, and closed her eyes. "It's funny."

"You know what's really funny?" he said.

She opened one eye. "What?"

"That you've lost your marbles."

"Oh, and there I thought you were going to say 'my virginity.'"

He chuckled darkly, hit the gas. "That, Olivia, I took a long time ago."

She placed her hand on his thigh. "Hmm" she murmured, as she splayed her fingers, inched them closer to his groin. He responded instantly, went rock hard under her touch, and he saw her smile to herself as she felt it.

"Be careful," he warned as he lobbed the Lamborghini into a tightening curve without fear, the tires holding their grip superbly. "You might get more than you bargained for."

"That a promise?"

He grinned, then turned onto a sandy road and wondered just how badly burned he was going to get before the job was done. He'd stepped over the line. But to hell with it. He loved her. Always had. And he was going to take what he could get, because he was pretty damn sure she wasn't going to want to see him again, once this was over. Ever.

And for the first time, fear whispered through Jack. Because now he had something to lose. And everything to gain.

The stakes had changed.

He felt her watching him again. "You know," she said seriously, "I think I prefer Henri to Jack. And he's certainly a lot more charming than Jacques."

A smile brushed his lips. But he said nothing. He knew what her father had to be thinking about "Henri" right about now.

"At least Henri allows you to smile," she said. "It looks good on you, you know."

"Not grim?"

"No, sexy. Crooked…but sexy. You should try it more often."

He focused on the road ahead, glad for his shades, for the way they were hiding his eyes and the way he was beginning to feel.

16:40 Romeo. Hamptons.
Wednesday, October 8.

The beach was empty at this time of year, especially in this weather. Cold wind stirred by another storm brewing off the coast, whipped froth off the waves and drove the tide high up the shore.

They walked in silence, thinking about everything that had happened here so many years ago, feeling the weight of lost time, of no time to lose, feeling the bite of salt and cold on their skin, the wet sand between their toes.

Olivia shivered and drew her down jacket close. Jack slipped his hand into hers. It seemed the natural thing to do. But neither wanted to speak, to give voice to their thoughts and break the spell, the strange sense that they were walking into the past, to a night sixteen years ago, to something neither of them had been able to properly confront. Something both still had to deal with. Together.

Jack led her away from the water and up through the dunes. He helped her up the bleached wooden stairs and onto the wide deck that fringed the entire house, the siding washed almost gray-white from salt wind and baking summer sun. It was getting dark. He brought out a blanket and the basket of food and wine. They sat in Adirondack chairs besides a portable outdoor heater. He placed the blanket around her shoulders, lit the gas and poured her a glass of deep-red wine.

Olivia sipped her wine as the sun set and night crept

over them. She stared out over the dune grasses at the dark void of ocean. The moon was visible between gaps in the rolling black cloud, and when it peeped through, ribbons of light stabbed through the glistening dark bellies of waves as they rose and curled over themselves before crumpling into foam and rolling to shore. The wine diffused warmth through her chest, and she felt more at ease, more safe with this man beside her than she'd felt in a decade and a half.

Being with him felt natural—as ordinary and as vital to her well-being as the simple act of breathing. How strange it was to slip so easily back into a relationship when so many unexplained years lay in between. She looked at him.

"Tell me about the Legion, Jack. What was it like?"

He took a sip of his wine, pursed his lips slightly. "It was a man's world. Deserts. Jungles. Guns."

She grinned. "Spoken like a true man. Where did you go on your tours?"

"Sahara, Congo, Cambodia, China, Malaysia…some places I can't mention."

"Or don't want to?"

"It's in the past."

"It must be tough to give up allegiance to your country, your family, every link to the past to join an army of foreigners like that." Her eyes narrowed. "Why would a man do that?"

"You know why I did it. Each man had his reason."

"I've heard that the bond between these men is so strong that they'll keep going with wounds in them the size of a fist to save a comrade, that they will stand in front of a firing squad without blindfolds—"

"You die for each other, not the country."

"That's the philosophy that you took to the FDS, isn't it?"

"It's become part of the fabric of who I am now. I will die for my men and they for me."

"And where would a woman fit in, Jack? Would your men choose allegiance over love? Is there even room for love in a life like that?"

He studied her from the darkness, the light from the lamp flickering over his features, shifting shadows so that she couldn't read him. "I don't know, Olivia," he said finally. "It's something each man may have to face in his own time. I can't speak for them on that count."

"What about you?"

He remained silent, sipped his wine. "This is a trick question, right?" he said finally.

Disappointment touched her. So that's how he was going to choose to deal with it.

"Do you think the end ever justifies the means, Jack?"

"You mean killing for money? It's a matter of perspective."

"I mean like using me to get to my father?"

He raised his brows slightly. "*Am* I using you, Olivia? I'm beginning to feel a little used myself, sexually speaking."

"I'm being serious here, Jack."

He sat silent for a while. "I'd have to say yes, that sometimes the end does justify the means. I think anyone who says otherwise is deluding themselves."

A strange sense of hurt and disappointment filled her. She didn't know why she was even pushing this, or what she hoped to gain from it. "What else should I expect from a mercenary," she said softly. "At least you're honest."

His eyes flashed to hers, and his body tensed slightly. "You think your father isn't a mercenary in the corporate sense? Look at what men like him do for power, for cash—they destroy lives. They just do it in a more removed fashion. They sit up there in their glass towers and pick up phones instead of guns. Don't judge me because I get my hands dirty, Olivia."

"I think we're talking about two different things here, Jack."

He sorted softly. "I'm not so sure." He reached for the bottle and topped off their glasses before setting it back on the little wooden table. "What's important is the end goal, Olivia, whether it's a good one or a bad one. Is it justifiable to sacrifice one innocent life in order to save millions more? Is it justifiable to take any life for personal power, capital gain?"

"Those moral lines aren't always so black-and-white, Jack."

"Yeah, they can get real gray—but that's my base point, that's how I weigh my actions. That's how I decide what battles my men will fight."

She leaned forward in her chair. "What's your *real* goal in the big scheme of things like life."

"To get you back, Olivia." He didn't even blink. His eyes held hers steady over the rim of her glass.

A dark thrill rippled through her. "Do you mean that?"

"I always say what I mean."

She stared at him, trying to read his eyes in the flickering interplay between light and dark. And an ominous thought threaded through her. Could this be the mercenary talking? Was this just another way of getting her to trust him? A way to ensure her betrayal of her father so that he could save all those innocent lives? She just couldn't be sure.

Olivia got up, went to the edge of the deck and leaned against the railing, holding her blanket close against the chill night wind. And her eyes began to sting as the weight of the years, of what he'd just said, seemed to be coming down on her.

Jack let her be for a few minutes. Hell, he didn't know why he'd said that. But, damn, it was true. He wanted her. It was the truest emotion in him. He'd tried to bury it all these years. He'd tried to let the iron gates of Fort de Nogent shut it out, tried to fight back in every physical way he could. But now he was here, back. And now he knew. *She* was his reason for being.

He watched her at the railing, her hair blowing softly in the wind. Then he tensed suddenly, every molecule in his body alert. He could sense something, a dark whisper in the breeze, something coming in with the bank of fog rolling on to shore. He'd developed the instincts of a predator—and a hunter could always sense another. It was the sixth sense he'd learned never to ignore.

He stood up, scanned the beach carefully. It was fully dark now and he couldn't see beyond the grasses, or into the mist moving in off the sea. It was coming in fast, swallowing the gleaming blackness of the waves, closing over the beach, moving up to the house.

Perhaps it was just her father's men out there, watching.

His FDS agent, McDonough, had them covered from the front of the house, and Davis was doing patrols round the back on the hour. But it suddenly didn't feel safe out here. He went to her at the railing. "Olivia—"

She turned to him and he saw that her eyes were glistening, like broken glass in moonlight. She looked so beautiful. The wine had softened her, made her eyes dreamy…and sad. Deeply sad. His heart cracked, and tenderness surged through him. At this moment he loved her more deeply and more violently than he could have ever dreamed possible. He'd kill anyone who tried to harm this woman. He'd tear them apart with his bare hands.

He glanced into the dank fog, that sense of unease, of being watched increasing. He cupped her face with his hand. "Come, Olivia, we need to go inside where it's warm."

And safe.

She hesitated. "What about the bracelet, Jack? Do you still feel you can't trust me enough to take it off?"

A sick feeling trickled through him. "Olivia," he said softly, "I *do* trust you. But it's for your protection. We need to know where you are if…anything goes wrong."

Something flickered in her eyes. "Like what, Jack?"

He looked into the mist again. "Nothing that we won't be able to take care of. Come."

00:59 Romeo. Hamptons beach.
Thursday, October 9.

The Zodiac caught the wave, surfed silently to shore. Seven men in black gear and balaclavas pulled the boat quickly up the beach. They left it just beyond the reach of the tide, hunkered down and ran softly over the sand, assault rifles ready.

Stopping near the dunes, the leader raised his hand, motioned with his fingers. The group split, three men taking the right flank of the big beach house, the other three scurrying left.

McDonough heard a noise. He stiffened, listened. But he could hear nothing more. He flipped down his night vision scopes, scanned the area, saw reeds moving in the wind, nothing else.

But his senses were now fully alert. He raised his hand, motioned for Davis to go do his sweep.

Chapter 10

01:00 Romeo, Hamptons beach house.
Thursday, October 9.

This time their lovemaking was slow, a tender coming together. Wind moaned up high in the rafters, the sound increasing as the storm closed in. Branches scratched against the windows, reeds rustled outside and surf crashed in the distance.

Jack had made sure the doors were locked, but the place was a security nightmare, with huge floor-to-ceiling glass windows everywhere. Even while he made love to Olivia, a part of his brain remained acutely aware of their surroundings. His gun was within arm's reach at all times. He knew exactly where his knife was, and he knew exactly what he was doing to Olivia.

This acuity of senses only sharpened his receptiveness to sensual pleasure.

A fire cracked and popped in the hearth of the sunken living room. The rugs under them were soft, and her lips tasted of salt.

Slowly he undressed her until she lay naked in front of him—apart from the silver bracelet, the gold liquid inside the capsule winking in the gleam of the fire. A grim reminder of the danger they faced.

He pushed open her thighs and slid his fingers into her, watching her eyes, feeling the way she opened wider for him, giving him access. She was warm, wet.

He closed his eyes, a small shuddering thrill running through his body, his groin growing hot, heavy. She reached up, undid his pants, and he swelled free in her cool hands.

Leaning over her, feeling the swell of her breasts against his chest, he nuzzled his face into her hair and entered her with a sharp thrust. She was slick, ready. A sweet pain sliced through his chest, stealing his breath. He pushed deep, burying himself in her, thrusting more urgently, desperately, a low moan of pleasure escaping him as sensation peaked in his body to a quivering, almost unbearable pitch.

But before he could release, she slid her thigh up along his torso, guiding him onto his back. She rolled on top of him, straddled him, and rode him, rhythmic strokes forcing her down onto him, making him go deeper, her muscles sucking on him, her breasts bouncing, her hair falling over her face like burnt amber in the firelight, until he could not hold back a second longer.

He exploded in violent release, and as he did, she spilled in waves of contractions over him, her body going rigid, her back arching as she cried out in primal pleasure.

She crumpled down onto him, with a small breathy laugh, aftershocks quivering through her body as he relaxed inside her.

He held her like that, lying on top of him, her hair falling softly over his cheek and his shoulder. He stroked her skin, savoring the exquisite sensation under his calloused hands. Her scent wrapped around him, her perfume, her sex. It was all so deliriously familiar, so utterly consuming, so welcoming. He felt as if his most secret dream had come alive right here in his arms. He felt as if he was back; he was home. He felt wholly Jack—not Jacques, not Henri, not any other alias he had ever played in his life. It was as if something broken at his center had knitted together again.

And it made him crave more, something that went beyond getting Killinger and his daughter and stopping the bombs. He wanted to finally be able to walk free in his own country, hold his head up high, be *proud* to bear his old name, the one he was rightfully born to—the one that had been stolen from him.

His eyes burned with emotion. He was going to succeed in this mission because it would exonerate him in the eyes of the nation—and in the eyes of the woman he loved.

She smiled suddenly and kissed him—a seductress with hair spilling over her face and creamy, naked shoulders. His heart swelled with a sweet hot ache and he grew hard all over again.

03:29 Romeo. São Diogo Island off Angolan coast.
Thursday, October 9.

A malignant shape crept through the São Diogo dune
flowers, moonlight catching snatches of ghostly skin,
the Atlantic rolling along the shore in the distance. He
drew the blanket from his cell higher over his head, hiding
his luminous hair. He felt no pain now. Just purpose.

He worked his way quietly toward the small white-
washed hospital and slipped behind a tangle of bougain-
villea as two nurses exited the building. They talked
softly in Portuguese.

He waited for them to disappear down the dune path,
then made his way in. There was only a skeleton staff
at this hour. It was quiet, dark. He found ICU easily.

The big man dwarfed the hospital bed, his dark skin
like ebony against sterile sheets. His eyes were closed, and
his body lay still, apart from the gentle rise and fall of his
chest with each mechanical hiss of the ventilator. He
knew now that this man's name was December. He was
one of the mercs responsible for his capture in Hamān and
subsequent torture. He knew this because he'd heard his
captors talking when they'd thought he was unconscious.

This man would be the first to pay.

03:29 Romeo. Hamptons beach house.
Thursday, October 9.

Olivia lay in Jack's arms, listening to the wind and
the rain that was now lashing at the windows, and felt
a dark fear growing inside her.

Perhaps it was just the way the temperature had plunged when the rain hit, or apprehension about what still lay ahead of them. Time was running out. It would be morning soon—another day closer to D-day.

She fingered the bracelet on her arm, and unanswered questions whispered through her mind.

She rolled on to her side, propped herself up on her elbow and looked down at him. "Jack, it doesn't make sense."

"Of course it does." He smiled his wickedly crooked smile and her heart lurched. "We make *perfect* sense."

"No, I mean this ultimatum you say the Cabal has given the president. What if Elliot *does* step down? Then this—"

He sat up, sighed, ruffled his hair brusquely with both hands. "I told you, he won't step down."

"How do you know?"

His face turned somber, and he watched her eyes carefully before answering. "The president is dying, Olivia."

Shock punched through her chest. "*What?*"

"He's being slowly assassinated by one of the prion variants from the Nexus Lab. It's eating through his brain like a fast-moving Alzheimer's and will ultimately cause severe dementia, then death. He's supposed to be dead already, Olivia, and Forbes was supposed to have already been sworn in as President under the 25th Amendment. But this particular prion variant has not yet been tested on humans. It's either not working to the timeline expected, or Elliot is a much stronger man—both physically and mentally—than the Cabal anticipated."

"I…I can't believe this. He's shown no evidence at all of being sick."

"He's doing his damnedest to hide it as long as he can, with Dr. Ruger's help. And if Elliot lives long enough to win this election, his running mate, Michael Taylor—the new vice president-elect—can take over when he dies. The Cabal and Forbes will have lost their window."

Olivia sat up and pulled the blanket tightly around her. "I…I can't believe this," she said again. "Can his illness be cured?"

He shook his head. "There's no antidote. The medical team on São Diogo is working 24/7 to develop one, but there's just not enough time, Olivia. His brain is already affected. The damage is irreversible. He *is* going to die."

An overwhelming sadness filled her. "He…he's such a good man, Jack."

"Yes, he is. He will not stop fighting, and *that*, Olivia, is why he will not step down."

"If they want him dead so urgently, why don't they just assassinate him another way, with a bullet or something?" she said with bitterness.

"Everything has to appear perfectly natural. It's part of the Cabal's long-term plan to win the confidence of the nation. If there is an overt assassination, there will be questions. Lots of them. There will be intense investigation. They can't afford any suspicion. It would destabilize their hold on power."

"What if we *can't* stop them before Monday, Jack? Surely Elliot would not allow those bombs to go off…to let so many people die. What would the Cabal have achieved then?"

He blew his breath out slowly. "Olivia, they're going to release the pathogen anyway."

She jerked to her feet, clutching the blanket over her breasts. "You cannot be serious! You mean this—" she waved her hand "—whatever it is we're doing now to stop the attack is for *nothing?*"

"No," he said calmly. "It's not for nothing. We will prevent huge loss of life by stopping the initial threat on the three major cities." He stood up, reached for his jeans, pulled them on. "Like I told you, the Cabal plan, once they have Forbes in power, is to launch the country into war. They will do this by releasing smaller amounts of pathogen, primarily to instill terror in the nation. The Cabal, through their new president Forbes, will accuse so-called terrorists and rogue nations of the acts. This will put Forbes in a legal position to retaliate with U.S. military force, and to launch preemptive strikes on oil-rich nations. The Cabal will effectively be sending the country into an era of violent expansionism the likes of which has not been seen since WWII. Cabal corporations in turn will be positioned to profit from this form of capitalistic imperialism."

He fastened the top button of his jeans.

"As a war-time president, Forbes will be granted sweeping powers under the constitution. This will put him in a position to initiate martial law, curtail civil liberties, and to postpone elections indefinitely. And then he will begin the slow process of appointing key Cabal puppets to top judicial, military, intelligence and business positions. For God's sake, the Senate is already Cabal-dominated." His eyes bored into hers.

"This, Olivia, amounts to a *coup d'etat*…and the end of democracy."

A strange unspecified panic tightened Olivia's chest. "Jack…I know my father. I mean…" She hesitated. "What is the actual proof you have that he is the one behind this?"

His brows shot up. "What you've seen is not enough?"

"It's…it's all circumstantial evidence, it's—"

"Circumstantial? Like it was against me all those years ago? Yet you chose to believe *my* guilt anyway."

"Jack, please, that's not fair. I—"

His eyes narrowed. "You're in denial, Olivia," he said. "Just like you were sixteen years ago."

"This is not about what happened back then. I'm only trying to understand how my father could possibly—"

"Yes, it *is* about what happened back then." A hint of hurt and frustration glinted in his eyes, but his voice remained level. "We all have our weak points, Olivia. I think yours is to run away from things you can't face. But you can't run away from this one. You can't pretend you need 'proof.' You know in your heart that your father is guilty. Just like I want to believe that you knew somewhere deep in your heart that I was innocent all those years ago."

He turned, took the two stairs up to the dining area and made his way to the kitchen. She watched him put the kettle on, his back strong, his muscles powerful. Yet inside he was wounded, scarred. By something *she* had done a long time ago. Or rather, hadn't done.

And this, she realized with a sinking heart, was why she was still wearing the bracelet. Jack might love her, but he still didn't—couldn't—trust her. He still wasn't sure of where she stood between himself and her father.

Olivia turned slowly to face the fire. She sat on the edge of the stone hearth and stared into the flames. And as she watched the mesmerizing play of orange over gold, her mind was taken back to another time, another fire—the fire on this very beach all those years ago.

Images flickered in and out of her consciousness like flames—Grayson with Elizabeth. Then Elizabeth leaving the fire, unsteady on her feet, wearing Jack's jacket.

Olivia tensed suddenly and her heart began to race. She had no idea that image even existed in her memory.

She held her head, as if doing so could force her mind back. Perspiration prickled over her body as a quick flash of Grayson stumbling after Elizabeth flared into her mind. Fear raced through her chest. *Had she blocked this?*

Her eyes shot to Jack over in the kitchen, his back to her. Her breathing became ragged. She'd buried this memory and it was coming free now because she was back here, in the same place, with Jack. Because being with him had awakened her deep inside.

Another bit of memory flashed in her mind—Jack, asking her if she'd seen Elizabeth, concern on his face, him mentioning he was worried about Grayson.

Oh, God. She put her hand to her mouth.

Was it true? Was this really her weakness? Did she have an ability to bury stuff like this and not even know she'd repressed it?

She thought of the therapist—her *father's* therapist. *He'd* brought him in. *He'd* instructed him to give her medication, sedation, hypnosis. To help her cope, they'd said. But perhaps their true intention had been to distort her perceptions of that night.

Smaller snatches of memory attached to the bigger images, dragged into her consciousness. She recalled her father coming into her room, his face grave, him telling her Jack was guilty. That was the word he'd used—*guilty*—even before the investigation. She remembered being introduced to the lawyers, all telling her she couldn't speak to Jack, that it would hamper Elizabeth's right to justice. They'd told her about the letter that had been found in his pocket…told her that Jack had been having sexual relations with Elizabeth. She remembered how this news had broken her, how she had crumpled, not wanted to live, how the doctor had then come in again and drugged her again. And…then Jack was dead, and the therapist told her she needed to put it all behind her and move on.

What had been the point of dwelling on his betrayal when he was gone and was never coming back?

Olivia tried to breathe as the realization overwhelmed her— *A whole chunk of her life had been a lie.*

And it was her fault. *She* was the one responsible for what happened to Jack. *She* could have fought back and helped him all those years ago. She should have seen through the deception. Through her own father's machinations.

Tears burned in her eyes as guilt and remorse flowed through her.

Jack was truly innocent. And she'd known it all along. She looked up. He was coming toward her with two mugs of steaming tea in his hands, his chest naked, his jeans worn in the most sinful of places.

Her heart buckled in pain—and love—for him.

She had to acknowledge her own guilt. She had to ask him if he could ever forgive her.

But as she was about to speak, his satellite phone vibrated with a dull buzz. He quickly set the mugs down, reached for it and scanned a text message.

His face changed as she watched him read the communiqué. His body grew hard, his muscles almost rippling with sudden adrenaline. His ice-gray eyes cut to hers—his scar pulling his mouth into a hard sneer.

Her heart stilled.

This was not Jack. This was a stranger. And she could see murder in his eyes.

"Go upstairs," he growled, his voice hard. "*Now.* Get dressed. Fast. Lock yourself in a room and do *not* move until I come for you."

Fear ripped through her "What is it, Jack?"

"Do it!"

They were surrounded by the enemy. Jack cursed violently as he hit McDonough's number. "How many out there?"

"Can't tell," his partner whispered. "Davis has gone around the south flank again. I'm going to come round the north side. And, Jacques…December is dead."

"I'll be ready." He hesitated. There was no time to

ask, to react, to mourn, but he had to know. "How did he die?"

"Our prisoner escaped, got to him in the hospital, pulled the plug on the ventilator."

Jack closed his eyes as rage ripped into his heart. But he didn't have time for grief—only vengeance. He found his control, opened his eyes. He could feel nothing now. Just lethal purpose, his mind focused like a laser.

He reached for his gun, strapped his knife to his ankle. He glanced up the stairs. Olivia should be safe up there. He pulled on his boots, flicked out the lights, waited in the darkness.

He heard the first gunshot.

Then another.

He positioned himself behind a central pillar of rough wood, listening.

He heard more gunfire, automatic, and almost simultaneously the huge picture window that faced the sea shattered in an explosion of sound and fell in a crumpling, clattering curtain of shards to the floor.

Then all was still, deathly silent, just cold wind intruding through the big black space where the window once hung. The fire flared up in the wind, tossing strange monster shadows at the walls.

Jack sensed a presence. More than one.

He took a step. Glass crunched under his foot. He stilled. He heard another movement, somewhere to his left.

He removed his knife from its sheath and breathed steadily, waiting.

A masked figure lurched out of the dark, the quick gleam of a knife in his hand.

Jack grabbed the knife arm, moved sideways, twisted and plunged his own blade where he knew damage would be lethal.

The man exhaled sharply, slumped over Jack's hand. Jack lowered the man to the floor quietly, yanked the knife free.

He moved toward the open window. He had no idea how many were out there, and who had been hit by gunfire—his men or theirs.

But he felt no fear. This was for December Ngomo, a fallen comrade. His death was somehow Samuel Killinger's fault. And no soldier of Jack's would die in vain.

There was a small rustle of movement to his side, inside the house. Jack spun around and fired, hitting the man as automatic fire went wide, ricocheting through the house.

Another man came at him from the back, fast. Turning, Jack met the assailant's charge with a violent blow to his throat. The man sagged to the ground, and Jack plunged his knife fast. He waited, listening for more men.

A scream ripped through the house.

Olivia!

He charged up the stairs in the dark, three at a time, feeling his way. He crashed open the door to her room.

The window was open. A white muslin curtain flapped in the storm wind, the rain pooling on the wood floor.

She was gone.

Chapter 11

05:00 Romeo. Hamptons beach house.
Thursday, October 9.

Jack flew to the window, looked down. A ladder reached up the wall. There was nothing below, just darkness, rain and thick swaths of swirling mist.

Then he heard another scream, carried on the wind, coming from the darkness near the water's edge. His heart turned ice-cold. *They were taking her by sea.* He should have seen it coming.

He slid down the ladder, hit the roof below, bounced off and rolled as he thudded onto hard sandy ground. He crouched in the reeds, orienting himself, the rain cold on his naked torso, the taste of water and salt in his mouth.

McDonough materialized at his side.

"They got Davis," he whispered.

Jack cursed bitterly. Two men in one night was two too many. He spoke through clenched teeth. "How many men out there?"

"Looks like four left. They came by water—they've got her down on the beach."

Jack assessed the situation quickly. "You take the right."

They hunkered down and ran quietly over the sand, the fog swallowing their approach. Jack could see the men now, dark shapes moving in and out of the swirling layers of blowing mist. Olivia was wearing white, a wraith between men in black from head to toe. She'd stopped struggling.

He told himself to relax. These men had to be her father's; they would not risk hurting her. They only wanted to get her out of the country. But he couldn't let them take her. If he lost Olivia, he would lose his only bargaining tool with Killinger. It would cost the mission.

And millions would die.

The rain was coming down harder now, lashing sideways at them. He gave McDonough a quick signal, and they moved fast, attacking in unison.

The assailants didn't know what hit them. Jack overpowered two men, killing them quietly. McDonough took care of the third man, leaving only one, who was now scrambling backwards toward the boat, dragging Olivia with him.

Jack walked straight toward him and Olivia.

The man glanced over his shoulder toward the boat, saw that he wouldn't make it. He hesitated, stopped, and positioned Olivia in front of him, pressing his gun to her temple. She remained deathly quiet, her eyes impossibly huge and dark against wet, pale skin. Rain glistened over her face, and her wet nightgown clung to every curve of her body, exposing her to these men.

"Back off," her captor ordered, "or I shoot her."

A quiver of violence speared through Jack. He forced himself to rein it in, stay focused. He said nothing. He kept walking slowly, steadily toward the man, his eyes locked on the man's face.

Her captor retreated slightly, pulling Olivia with him. "I said back off or she dies!"

Jack could hear the fear in the man's voice, and this fed him. He went right up to him, knowing the man could not run, because Jack would shoot and kill him before he made it two feet. He also knew Killinger would probably kill the man himself if Olivia was harmed.

Jack reached the man, raised his gun, held his arm straight, and pushed the muzzle against the man's forehead. "Let her go," Jack growled, angling his weapon hard into the man's temple. "Or *you* die."

McDonough stood silent, watching, ready.

"I...I'll kill her," the man warned.

"You won't hurt her. She's wanted alive, not dead."

"I'll do it, I swear."

"Then you will die anyway. Let her go and you might see another day."

The man released Olivia, very slowly, and McDonough lurched forward and grabbed her away.

Jack looked into the man's eyes and squeezed the trigger.

"Jack!" Olivia shrieked in horror. She broke free of McDonough's hold and stumbled wildly up the beach toward the house. McDonough started to run after her.

"Let her go," Jack yelled as he watched her stagger over the sand toward the house. He felt sick to his stomach.

Olivia was never going to feel the same about him now.

He dropped to his haunches, checked the man's pockets. McDonough joined him and began searching the others.

Jack pulled out ID, shone his flashlight on one of the cards. McDonough came to his side. "Looks like they're all Venturion Security," he said grimly. "They're Killinger's men."

Jack nodded and stared up the beach, in the direction she'd run. "I should've seen this coming," he whispered. "She told Killinger she'd be in Los Angeles in six days. Kidnapping his own daughter was his last resort, the only way to get her safely out of the country. Hell, I'd have done it myself."

McDonough was studying him quietly, rain glistening over his face. "You knew her from before, didn't you?"

Jack's eyes cut to McDonough. Only McBride, Zayed and Ngomo had been privy to that information. "Yeah," he said slowly. "How'd you know?"

McDonough was silent for a while, just the sound of surf crunching in the mist and wind. "First time I've ever seen you get riled like that."

Jack cursed softly.

"Go to her," said McDonough. "I'll call for backup, take care of this."

"Where's Davis?"

"Round the side of the house. He took a bullet in the head. It was quick, Jacques."

Jack nodded, remorse, bitter and foul, filling his mouth "It's Jack," he said through his clenched jaw. "That was my name. Jack Sauer." He didn't have to say it. But it came from his gut anyway. It was as if he needed to reclaim the past for himself if he was to go up to that beach house to try and reclaim Olivia. Especially in the face of what she'd just seen him do. "We were engaged. Once."

"Go to her," McDonough said. "She needs you. I'll handle this."

Jack stood, slapped the man on the shoulder, and held it for a moment. McDonough nodded.

And Jack ran up the beach after Olivia.

He found her sitting in a crumpled wet ball on the deck stairs, sobbing, rocking.

"Olivia—" He touched her shoulder gently.

"Get away from me!" She yelled as she jerked away and jumped to her feet. Mascara streaked her pale cheeks, and her hair stuck in wet strands over her face. "I don't know you, Jack! I...I thought I did. I thought that maybe you were still the same inside. But you're not." She whirled around and staggered inside, over the broken glass. A shard cut into her foot and she sucked her breath in sharply, but she kept on going, limping into the living room, toward the fire, toward warmth.

Jack followed her into the house, his boots crunching on glass as he turned on the lights. She'd left a trail of bloody footprints over the wood floor, and his heart twisted violently at the sight of it. It was a primal reaction, not a sensation he could articulate, just a fiercely protective reflex…couched in anger. He'd lost Ngomo, Davis. And now he was losing Olivia.

She sat next to the fire, huddled over, shivering.

He went to her, lifted his hand to touch her, aching to feel her, to envelop her in his arms and hold her tight against his chest.

She whirled to face him, raising both hands in warning. "Don't—" her voice was hoarse, cracked "—don't touch me again. Ever."

This was his fault. He'd been too damn busy loving her, too damned involved in his own emotions to have picked up on the warnings in time. Even McDonough had noticed his loss of control. He cursed himself. He should've stood guard instead of making love. Guilt swamped him. And now she was lost to him.

And not only that, but now the mission was in jeopardy.

"Olivia," his voice was flat. "I *need* to touch you— I need to look at your foot."

She glanced down, almost surprised to see her own blood.

"You're in shock, Olivia. You're not thinking straight. I'm going to find you a blanket, get you warm. And I must stop that foot from bleeding."

She raised her eyes to meet his. "You killed him, Jack. I know you're a mercenary—I know sometimes you take lives, but this…this was in cold blood."

"I *saved* you, Olivia."

"You gave him an ultimatum. He let me go, and *then*

you shot him." Her voice cracked. "You shot him in the head. Point-blank. Right there. Just like that."

He fell silent for a while, just watching her, struggling to find the right words, trying to get a grip on the aftereffects of adrenaline and testosterone still humming through his body.

"Olivia," he said finally. "I couldn't let him live. We can't leave *any* loose ends. It would jeopardize the mission."

"The *mission?* What the hell happened to you, Jack? What happened to the things you used to believe in?"

His gut twisted. He took a step toward her. "They killed *my* man out there Olivia."

"Doesn't give *you* the right to kill them."

His voice grew cool, measured. "Yes, I gave that guy an ultimatum, just like *your* father gave President Elliot and his nation an ultimatum. And yes, then I shot him. Just like your father will *still* launch the bio attacks and kill millions of innocent people. Olivia, that man was *not* innocent." He came even closer, his voice going lower. "There are no rules in this war."

She shook her head in raw disbelief. "There is *never* justification for *murder,* Jack."

"Tell that to your father." He paused. "Do you know why those men wanted you? Have you even thought about that?"

Confusion, then fear, touched her eyes.

"They're your *father's* men, Olivia."

He let it sink in.

"They came under *his* orders, prepared to kill to get you safely out of the country before he launches the attacks." He cursed softly under his breath. "Your father fights dirty, Olivia. But he's met his match, because I can play dirty, too."

"Revenge is—"

"Enough." He cut her off, his tone brooking no further debate. "I need to fix your foot, and we need to get out of here before the cops arrive."

Olivia stared in shock as Jack, still shirtless, the blood of another man on his torso, moved coolly around her house, cleaning himself up as he searched for first-aid supplies.

She glanced at the big void where the window once was, the glistening glass shards all over the wooden floor, and she shuddered violently with the horror of what had just happened.

She could flee. Out that window. His words snaked into her mind. "We all have our weak points, Olivia…yours is to run away from things you can't face…. You can't run away from this one."

But she wanted to. Desperately. Her eyes shot to the staircase. Her shoes were upstairs…if she could get to them before he came out of the bathroom—

Too late. He appeared from the doorway, towels and medical supplies in hand.

"Take that nightgown off," he said as he set the supplies next to her.

She blanched, suddenly insanely vulnerable. This was a man she didn't understand anymore.

"Come on, Olivia, the clock's ticking. You need to dry off, warm up, and we've got to get out of here."

She lifted the sodden fabric slowly over her head and stood naked in front of him, feeling incredibly exposed. But there was no sexual interest in his eyes. No kindness, either.

Yet there was still tenderness in his touch as he wrapped a blanket gently around her. She drew it tight around her shoulders and watched him stoke the fire. This man was an enigma to her. One minute he was a warm and incredibly attentive lover with whom she wanted to spend the rest of her life, and in the next he was a cold-blooded killer.

Jack Sauer may not have murdered Elizabeth all those years ago, but the forces that had shaped him during his exile had turned him into a man who was capable of acts she could never condone.

He crouched in front of her, placed her foot in his lap and began to pull out pieces of glass, sopping up blood that welled from the cuts.

He concentrated intently on his task, his big, rough hand working the delicate tweezers with dexterity and speed. He found the large shard he was after, tugged. It came free and he released it into a saucer he'd placed at his side. It hit the china with a clink.

Olivia stared at the bloody piece of glass, the pain in her foot almost a welcome diversion as he dug back into her skin, trying to grasp another sliver. Pain made her feel real somehow. It gave her something safe to focus on.

She watched his head, the way his wet hair glistened like ink in the firelight. She thought about the silver streaks he'd covered with the dye. It reminded her of how much time had passed between them, and how differently they might have grown had they been to-gether. A strange sadness ached in her.

He glanced up. "You okay?"

She nodded, tears suddenly threatening her eyes. What was happening to her? She was a mess. She couldn't think straight anymore. She didn't even know how to be consistent in her feelings for this man.

Her phone chimed and she jumped in fright.

They looked at each other, then at her purse on the table where the noise was coming from.

He set her foot down gently, scooped the purse up and brought it over to her. He held it out. The phone rang again. Her heart quickened and her eyes shot to his.

"Take the call," he said softly.

She took her purse, opened it, removed her phone and checked the incoming number. It was her father. And this time she knew why he was calling. Indecision froze her.

"Answer it, Livie," he said as he crouched back down in front of her.

She swallowed against the pinch in her throat and put the phone to her ear. But she'd lost her ability to speak. She couldn't even say hello to her own father.

"Olivia?"

"Yes," she managed to whisper.

Her dad was strangely silent for a moment. "Are you okay?"

She took a deep, shuddering breath. "No, I'm not. Some men just tried to abduct me."

Jack's eyes flashed up to hers, and his body tensed, ready to snatch the phone from her.

"Oh God, are you hurt? What happened?"

"Henri…rescued me."

Jack relaxed visibly, picked up her foot again, began to swab it with cold disinfectant.

"Where are you, Olivia—where did this happen?"

He knew damn well where she was. This farce was going too far. Bitterness leached into her chest. "I'm at the beach house."

"Tell me exactly what happened, Olivia."

"I'm not sure," she said, her voice growing stronger, colder. "All I know is that Henri and his men saved me."

"His *men?*"

Jack dried her foot, his eyes fixed on her face.

"He travels with bodyguards."

Her father sighed heavily. "Do you know *why* he travels with bodyguards, Olivia? He's a black market arms dealer. He's a dangerous man with questionable connections, and I don't want you around him. Whoever tried to abduct you was probably trying to get to him. He has enemies, Olivia. And people who cross Henri Devilliers disappear."

"So you checked up on him?"

"Of course I checked him out."

She felt her heart go numb.

"Have…have you been to the police, sweetheart?"

"No."

"It's probably better that you don't. I want to know exactly what this Devilliers is involved in. I'll send my own people to look into it. In the meantime, I want you to come home."

She closed her eyes. Her father was a bold-faced liar.

He wanted to cover this up, just like he wanted to cover up who really killed Elizabeth.

"I'm not coming home. Henri can keep me safe."

She watched as Jack taped adhesive sutures to her cut. Her father was silent, for too long, but she was beyond trying to bridge the gap.

Finally he spoke and she heard the shift in tone. "I want to meet this man."

"Yes," she said. "He wants to meet you, too." She felt nothing in saying it. She was playing the charade now, fully, being a traitor—a mercenary—just like him, just like Jack. They were all the same now—all three playing their parts to their own ends.

"Can he postpone his L.A. business for a few days, perhaps join us on the yacht?"

This was it—this is what Jack wanted from her. This is where her father needed her to be. She could feel the circle closing in. "I'll ask him."

She lowered the phone, held her hand over it. "My father wants to know if we will both join him on his yacht on the thirteenth."

Jack nodded his head slowly, something unreadable in his eyes, the stress muscle throbbing at his jaw line.

She cleared her throat. "He says it can be arranged."

"I'm delighted to hear it, I'll see you then, sweetheart. Let…Henri know it's formal attire."

She hung up and began to shake.

Jack scooped her into his arms held her tight. She couldn't feel anything, just cold. She felt distant from both Jack and her father. She felt strangely isolated from herself.

Jack released her. "You feel any warmer?"

"Yes," she lied.

His eyes softened. "Go up and get dressed," he said gently. "I need to organize a few things with my guys, then we head straight for the airport."

Olivia climbed the stairs, reached the top, heard him begin talking on his phone. She edged behind the wall, listened.

"We're in—I have an invitation from Killinger. Affirmative, we leave for the Caribbean ASAP. Have the jet fueled and pilot on standby at JFK…no, I don't think we need the chopper rental, we'll use the day to drive up. I could use the time with her. Yeah…I have her trust, but I'm worried about the final showdown. I need to work on her a bit more, just to be sure. Okay, we'll go over strategy on the plane."

I need to work on her a bit more.

Anger leached into Olivia's chest. She was a pawn. Plain and simple. She clenched her teeth and fisted her hands at her sides. These two men in her life might love her, and she might love and hate them both in a fierce cocktail of emotions she couldn't even begin to articulate, but the black reality was that they would both probably sacrifice her for a higher purpose. She could see that now.

She was on her own, and she'd do well to remember that. She wasn't going to be played, not anymore.

Chapter 12

16:00 Romeo. Road to Manhattan.
Thursday, October 9.

They stopped at a coffee shop on the way back to New York. Jack ordered sandwiches, but Olivia wasn't hungry.

She stood apart from him, trying to keep weight off her sore foot. Behind the counter, a television screen was set to the CBNN twenty-four-hour news channel. She looked up, caught sight of President Elliot's face. Her heart accelerated. The camera cut to a close-up of Dr. Ruger.

Olivia moved away from Jack, leaned over the counter. "Could you turn that up?"

The server reached behind her and bumped up the sound. The news anchor was talking now. *"White*

House spokesman Andy Fischer has denied allegations that the president is ill. Speculation about the commander in chief's health, however, continues…"

Olivia felt the blood drain from her head. She glanced at Jack. He was waiting in line to pay. She looked at the television again.

"Veteran Elliot-watcher Mel Berkowitz is with us in the studio this morning. Mr. Berkowitz, how do you think this will affect the campaign…"

Olivia placed her hands on the counter, as if it would stop her world from tilting further. This was real. This was here in this coffee shop, on this television, real people watching, everyday people. Innocent people.

Her father had done this.

Her eyes shot to Jack. There were still two people in the lineup in front of him. She wanted nothing to do with this…with him. Or her father.

She swiveled on her heels, pushed the door open, stepped into the fresh air and let the mist of fine rain kiss her face. She began to walk, and she kept on walking, right through the parking lot, past the Lamborghini, across the street, cars swerving around her and honking as she went. She didn't care. She just kept walking, faster and faster.

Jack hurried the cashier as he watched Olivia through the window. He picked up the coffee and sandwiches, phone to his ear. "You got her covered, Mc-Donough?"

"Yeah, want us to bring her in?"

"No. Don't touch her," he said, pushing the door open with his shoulder. "She's cracking. If we lose her now, we won't get onto that yacht. Just keep an eye on her. I'll take care of it."

He put the coffees and sandwiches into the car, got in, fired the ignition.

He caught up to her heading down a side road. He turned in, drove slowly up behind her. She wasn't limping anymore, she was numb, walking right through her pain, both mental and physical.

He cursed softly, tension mounting in him. This was not good. He drew up alongside her and opened the door. "Get in, Olivia."

She gave no indication she'd even heard him, she just kept on going, her face deathly pale, fine rain sparkling like diamonds in her thick chestnut hair. He cursed again, wound down his window, drove slowly behind her, tires crackling on the wet surface, the wipers snicking over the windscreen. "Olivia—"

She walked faster, her breath misting in the cool air.

He pulled out into the road, drove ahead, stopped the car, got out. He walked back to her, placed his hands on her shoulders, halting her. He held her still. "Olivia," he said gently.

She pushed him away. "Please, just get away from me, Jack." She spun round and stalked off in the other direction.

He grabbed her arm, jerked her around. "Olivia—"

"Let me go!" She had a wild look in her eyes.

"Olivia, please, will you get in the car. We can talk—"

She held out her arm. "Just take this thing off me, Jack, and let me go!"

"Where to? Where do you want to go?"

"I don't know! I just…I just want out."

He had to make her think, logically, rationally. "Out from what, Olivia?"

"You. My dad. Grayson. The past. This…this thing." She held out her wrist, moisture filling her eyes. "I can't play this game. I can't do this, Jack. I'm not like you."

"You *have* to do this, Olivia."

Tears ran down her cheeks and mingled with the rain. "He's my father! Dammit, Jack, I love him. How am I supposed to accept he's a terrorist? How…how am I supposed to live with *that?*"

He tightened his grip. "That, Olivia, is *why* you have to do this. You are the only one who can get me close to him. You can't back out of this now."

"I want to talk to him. I want to ask him why…why he tried to destroy you all those years ago, why he hurt me—" Her voice cracked. "A whole chunk of my life has been a damn lie. Do you realize that? I…I thought I was a strong person, Jack." Her tears were streaming now. "I thought *I* was in control of my life. I'm not. I never was. *He* was controlling me. He…he took *you* from me. I don't want any part of this anymore. I just want out. I want myself back.… I…don't even know who I am anymore."

He held her steady. "Look at me, Livie, look into my eyes. You *have* to stop running." He cupped her face in both hands, forcing her to keep looking into his eyes. "Remember that Congo footage? Remember what happened to those infected with the pathogen?"

Her bottom lip wobbled.

"You do not have a choice, Livie, and neither do I. You *are* part of this. So am I. Our pasts are tied into the future. We can't walk away. We *have* to see this through to the end."

She stared at him, rain and tears glistening on her face.

He softened his voice. "Livie, I *know* you. You're about justice. And so am I."

She glanced away. "I just don't want to believe that he's done this," she whispered.

"Don't let him finish it, then. Save him from that ultimate sin. *Help* him."

Her eyes searched his deeply as if looking for answers he couldn't give. How did one explain the betrayal of a parent?

"Come," he said gently, "let's get in the car."

She let him lead her in.

Jack started the vehicle, his heart pounding. He'd finally broken her down.

But he'd almost gone too far, and the taste it left in his mouth was one of bitterness and remorse, not victory.

The rain lashed at them as they neared the city, and the sky hung gray and low, the somber weather outside reflective of how Olivia felt inside. Jack had put the top of the car up, and the windows were streaked with shivering rivulets of rain. She stared at them, watching the world fly by, her past unraveling.

Jack was right. She did run from things.

She could face all manner of horrors in her job, but when it came to personal demons, she buried her head in the sand.

Did that make her weak?

Even the strongest man had at least one pivotal

weakness, a vulnerability the rest of the world might never see, yet it often shaped who he was, even fired his strength. Her father had once told her that. How much, she wondered, had been in reference to himself?

She glanced at Jack, his profile so rugged, his strong hands so relaxed on the wheel, so in control. He was like a rock, the one constant in her life. "What do you think my father's greatest weakness is, Jack?" she asked.

He cocked a brow in surprise. "Guilt."

"Guilt?"

"Yeah. Over your mother's death."

"I don't see how his remorse over that accident so long ago is his weakness now."

"You, Olivia, are the living symbol of what Samuel Killinger lost that night by driving too fast. You look just like your mother. You're the last living bit left of her. Your father is so possessed by this notion that he has tried to control your life, contain you so that he can protect you. He will do almost anything to ensure your well-being, and that gives us something to use against him."

Her jaw dropped. "When on earth did you get to be so psychoanalytical?"

He grinned. "I didn't. That's what our profiler came up with, using the information we gave her."

"You have a profiler?"

"Yes, Dr. Emily Carlin, here in Manhattan. We give her the info she needs, she does her thing, provides us with a report, and then we decide how to move—on certain leaders of state, for example. Knowing how a dictator's mind works can really help shape military strategy."

"Did you have her profile me?"

He shot her a look and chuckled. "Nope. That I managed all by myself."

She studied his face. What had her father put this beautiful man through? What had *she* put him through? What had to have been going through his mind during that time? He'd only been twenty-three. On the run, alone, accused of murder—one of the most powerful, albeit clandestine, groups in the country trying to make sure he went down for it.

And she'd deserted him.

A rawness ripped through her, so powerful it twisted her features and flooded her eyes instantly. She took a deep breath of air.

It was time to pick sides and stand firm. It was time to do the right thing.

It was time to stop running.

"Jack?"

He glanced at her, saw her face and pulled over instantly. Concern touched his eyes. "What is it, Livie?"

"Jack… I am so, so sorry." It was all she could say. How could you put what she felt into words? The utter remorse, the regret. "I'm sorry I wasn't there for you. I am sorry I never…I am sorry—"

He placed the palm of his hand against the side of her face, looked deep into her eyes, something so incredibly dear and gentle in his own. She didn't need the words. She didn't need to tell him. He understood. She could see it in his eyes.

"Can you ever forgive me?"

"You need to forgive yourself, Olivia," he said softly.

Tears rolled hot down her cheeks. "I love you, Jack. So much."

His own eyes glistened sharply. The corner of his lip twitched. Rain beat down on the soft roof. Traffic rumbled by.

"I've always loved you, Olivia," he whispered, leaning closer. "I never stopped loving you."

"But I betrayed you. I let you down."

"It hurt."

"Can you understand…what happened to me?"

He sucked in a deep breath, looked away for a second. "I don't know." He turned back. "Can you?"

She bit her lip. His answer hurt incredibly. She *needed* him to understand.

"Maybe some things can never be understood. Maybe they just need to be accepted. And maybe then we can move on."

She nodded.

"We've both been given a second chance here. It's what happens next that matters. That will be our test."

"What *will* happen on the yacht, Jack?"

Something moved like ink through his eyes, and his features shifted again. So did the tone of his voice. "Do you trust me?"

Unease tightened her chest. "I…I'm not sure I like the way you said that, Jack."

"I *need* you to trust me, Olivia." The intensity in his voice was alarming.

Nerves skittered through her stomach. "Yes," she

whispered. "I trust you. I believe in you. I...I've picked my side, Jack. I'm in your hands, now."

He kissed her hard and desperately on the mouth.

18:02 Romeo. JFK.
Thursday, October 9.

He checked his watch. The time difference had gained him almost a day on the flight over from São Diogo. He pulled out a stool, seated himself at the bar, dialed the private line he used to communicate with Samuel Killinger.

Killinger picked up instantly. "Yes?"

He heard the uncertainty, the nerves, and pleasure rippled through him. He'd surprised the man.

"It's me."

"I...thought you were caught up in the unrest in Hamān."

He thought about his torture at the hands of the FDS, the dank cell. "You could say that I was caught up."

"Why are you calling? You want the payment transferred?"

He remained silent, tightening the tension, playing his prey. "No," he said finally. "The job is incomplete. Dr. Sterling is still alive."

"*What!* Where is she?"

He could hear him breathing. "We need to talk. In person."

"We never meet in person."

He could hear fear now. He knew Samuel Killinger didn't want anyone to know about his personal assassin. Killinger didn't want his colleagues to know he'd had his own Venturion board members taken out from time to time.

"You're messing with me. It's imperative that I know at once where she is. This…could have grave implications. Tell me, and you will get your fee, regardless."

"They've taken her to an island off Africa."

"Who?"

He motioned to the bartender as he spoke, pointed to a bottle of tequila. "I think there's more at stake here than you allowed me to believe, Killinger. It almost cost me my life in Hamān. I do not like being used. I need full knowledge of a situation before I go in to do a job. You played me for a fool. I don't appreciate it."

"Fine, we'll renegotiate. But we cannot meet in person. It's out of the question."

"Hmm, a matter of national security, perhaps?"

Dead silence. "All right—when do you want to meet?"

The bartender placed his drink in front of him. He nodded in thanks, picked up the glass, swigged it back, felt the heat. He was glad for it. It would help dull the pain of the torture still lingering in his body. He motioned for another. He'd heard his captors talking outside his cell on São Diogo, before he'd escaped and killed the man they called December. They'd mentioned a deadline of October 13 more than once. They'd also mentioned a gathering on Killinger's yacht. It sounded important.

"I can see you on the thirteenth," he said, fishing. "Not before."

Killinger swore.

The man smiled. Killinger never swore. And he himself rarely smiled. Killinger had played him, and he was going to play him back. Every now and then he enjoyed indulging in a game like this.

"I'll be in the Caribbean on that day."

He nodded to himself. "Where will you be staying?"

"I'll be on my yacht. We can meet there. I need to see you before eleven that night. Any later will be of no use to me, and you can forget your fee."

"The name of your yacht?" He knew already. He'd made it his business to know everything about the people who hired him to kill.

"The *Genevieve*."

"Your wife's name. Very nice."

Silence.

"She looks so much like your wife."

"Who?"

"Olivia." He hung up, sucked back his tequila, the movement tearing at the injury in his neck where the sultan had stabbed him.

Killinger stared at the cell phone in his hand. His chest was tight, squeezing his lungs like a vise. He was losing control. If Paige Sterling was alive, it meant someone had gone to a great deal of trouble to fake her death. Either someone was on to his plan or would be soon.

Had President Elliot broken the silence? Had he managed to enlist someone who was operating out there in the shadows, working against him?

He thought of Henri Devilliers and his shady connections. Was *he* involved in some way?

He tried to breathe. He had to release the pathogen now. He had no other choice.

He walked to his window, still gripping his phone. But Olivia was out there somewhere, out of his grasp. He had no antidote near her, no one to whisk her out of the country. He *had* to wait.

What would it all be worth if he killed his own daughter? What kind of man would that make him?

He clenched his jaw, thinking.

He turned suddenly, picked up his other phone and began punching in a series of codes that would set off a chain of events that only he personally would be able to halt.

He hung up, feeling a resurgence of his power. He had just initiated protocol that would cause the bombs to blow at precisely five minutes past midnight on October 13, Eastern standard time. He had just bought himself additional bargaining power—insurance—in case things went sideways.

If all went according to plan and Elliot stepped down before midnight as planned, he would press the button that would deactivate the code of instructions. If not, the pathogen would release—with or without him.

And it was time to end his relationship with his albino assassin. He would have his guards take him down, on the yacht, nice and quiet down in the hold.

He'd do the same with Devilliers as soon as he could lure Olivia away from him.

He'd find a way to explain the man's disappearance to Olivia. And she'd get over it, just as she'd gotten over Jack Sauer all those years ago.

He stilled in mild shock. Why was he even *thinking*

about Jack Sauer? He frowned, stared out his windows at the lashing rain and the gray sky.

It was because of Devilliers, that's why. There was something vaguely haunting about the man. His daughter was clearly attracted by a certain type.

06:30 Romeo. Over the Atlantic.
Friday, October 10.

"Wake up, princess." He couldn't help it, she looked like one to him, rumpled and sexy in his bed on the FDS jet, miles above the world. More than once he'd glanced up from his desk and had to fight the urge to climb into that bed beside her. But he had work to do. He had to coordinate the takedown. They now had fewer than four days to stop Killinger.

She sat up, pushed her lustrous mane of hair off her face, her eyes dreamy, and she smiled sleepily at him. His stomach swooped instantly—no air turbulence involved—and he felt himself go rock hard.

"Hey, your eyes…they're gray again."

"Giving them a break from the contacts." He winked as he spoke.

She went silent, her eyes holding his.

Jack swallowed at the electricity beginning to hum between them.

"I missed you, Jack."

The words were so simple, yet they held so many layers, covered so many years. He smiled back at her, a strange sadness welling his heart. "I missed you too, Livie," he whispered. *More than you will ever know.*

She held out her hand to him.

He took it, sat on the bed beside her. She touched his mouth where the scar met his lips.

"I love it when you smile, you know?"

"And I love it when you sleep in my bed." He squeezed her hand. "And now you better get dressed before I get in there with you. We land in half an hour."

Her face turned serious. She glanced at the table, his papers, his laptop, his phone. "You've been busy."

He nodded. "Been putting together a shopping list."

She cocked a brow. "What for—assault rifles and grenades?"

He laughed. "No, weapons of a different kind. Henri and his lady like to dress in high style. We need to get ourselves a couple of killer outfits, my dear."

She raised the other brow. "You're serious."

He narrowed his eyes in jest. "Deadly serious. We have a challenging cover to maintain—lovers in the Caribbean."

She laughed, and her eyes turned grave almost instantly. "He'll have men waiting for us when we land, won't he?"

Jack nodded. "They'll be picking up our tail again, for sure. But FDS will have men, too."

"What about this plane, won't they trace it?"

"Probably. It's registered to a company that belongs to Henri Devilliers, which they will discover if they look hard enough. Otherwise, they'll find nothing at all. The cover is tight. And it must remain so until we are on that yacht."

A shiver ran through her.

He touched her cheek. "You'll be fine, Olivia."

Doubt pooled in her eyes. She glanced at the metal cuff on her wrist.

Guilt oozed in him. He looked away, started to head toward the cockpit.

"Jack, wait. Will you please take this off?"

He sighed deeply, turned to face her. "I'm sorry, Olivia."

Disappointment stole into her features. "You still don't trust me, do you? You think I won't be able to stand up to my father when I see him."

"I do trust you."

"Then take this off."

"Olivia, the *only* reason that's on now is for your own protection," he lied, looking right into those clear honey-gold eyes. His chest constricted so tightly it hurt. "There's been one kidnap attempt already. If it happens again, the GPS in that cuff will enable us to find you. You do understand that, don't you?"

Her eyes remained locked onto his. "Why would my father try that again? I'm out of the country."

"He might not want Henri on his yacht. If he is nervous enough, he might try and separate us before Monday."

Her mouth flattened, and she averted her eyes.

Jack went to the cockpit, his fists balling at his sides. He'd broken her down, he'd rebuilt her trust. And now he was going to have to smash it to smithereens.

To get Killinger, to save the nation, he was going to have to pay the ultimate sacrifice—he was going to have to kill his dream.

He was going to have to give Olivia up for good.

Chapter 13

The White House correspondent speed-dialed the CBNN producer's direct line. The producer picked up on the first ring. He'd clearly been expecting the call.

"Something major is going down," said the correspondent. "The president has called a press conference for tonight."

"What time?"

"That's what's really weird—eleven-thirty."

The producer whistled softly. "His health?"

"That's my guess. He's clearly not well…" He hesitated, glanced over his shoulder. "My contact told me Elliot was slurring his words this morning, and he stumbled twice. I…I think he might actually invoke the twenty-fifth."

"Christ! I'll get things rolling…."

17:00 Romeo. Grand Cayman.
Monday, October 13.

The late-afternoon Caribbean sun was warm on his naked torso as it sank toward the horizon, tinting the sea a shimmering copper. Today was the day. In seven hours it would all be over.

Jack paced the length of their private balcony as he talked on the phone, his languid motion belying the gravity of his discussion.

His first call had been to check on December's funeral arrangements.

His next call was to the FDS dive boat. The vessel was chugging out from a cove in Little Cayman at this very moment, setting course for the *Genevieve*, masquerading as a tourist dive charter. Another craft was approaching the *Genevieve* from the north—this one disguised as a deep-sea fishing charter.

The choppers were on standby on Little Cayman. They'd be in the air and approaching the *Genevieve* shortly before midnight. The team he'd moved out of Honduras was also in position, strategically distanced from the Killinger yacht

Jack signed off and set his phone down on the glass-topped table where hotel staff had put the drinks and snacks he'd ordered. He picked up the printout and studied the specs for the *Genevieve* again, committing the layout to memory.

The motorized yacht was a monstrosity, complete with twenty-six state rooms and a helipad that would play nicely into their strategy. Killinger's office was off the main stateroom on the port side, according to Olivia.

He set the specs down, cracked open a cold beer, turned to look over the sea and sipped. The necessary weapons had been procured from their Honduras operation. He had his personal weapons with him, but they were mostly for show, since he expected he'd be frisked upon embarking the *Genevieve*. Killinger would be surprised if Henri was not packing, and he'd take care to disarm him.

His real weapon was the detonator tag and the cuff around Olivia's arm. He was now wearing the detonator on a chain around his neck, just as if it were a military dog tag. The syringe and antidote had been installed into a compartment in his shoe, thanks to McDonough.

Jack walked up to the edge of the balcony, placed his beer on the balustrade and inhaled deeply as he thought about that aspect of the operation. The medics were on standby with the choppers. If necessary, they could get Olivia to a hospital within minutes. She'd be safe. But still, he didn't like the idea. Not one bit.

For too many reasons to count.

He stared over the sea, trying to moderate the unusual adrenaline pumping through his body.

Once the operation was complete, authorities would be notified and the FDS would move out. It would be best to eliminate Killinger in the takedown—a man with his power and connections was not easily contained behind bars. It would be simple enough to take him out with a stray bullet, and the world would be a safer place. But Jack knew now he could never do that to Olivia.

The man might be amoral, highly powerful and dangerous, but he was still her father. If he killed Killinger tonight, Olivia would hold it against him forever. He'd hold it against himself.

They were going to have enough against them as it was—after tonight a future for the two of them might never be possible.

He snagged his beer, swigged deeply.

Olivia stepped out of the shower and toweled off. Her body felt good—warmed from the sun, salted by hours in the sea and sated from an afternoon of making slow and languorous love as waves had rolled in to the shore outside and a soft Caribbean breeze had billowed the muslin drapes in their room.

She smoothed lightly scented lotion over her body, noting she'd already picked up a light tan. She examined the new bikini lines made by the skimpy little thing Jack had picked out for her, and smiled.

They'd spent most of yesterday shopping—him sitting in dressing rooms, her parading one outfit after another. He'd finally selected the sleek body-hugging backless gown she would wear tonight. It was a bold choice in blood red—one Henri would have made, he'd said. But she'd seen in his eyes that Jack Sauer himself very much approved.

Later they'd laughed and dined under palms overlooking the sea. They'd walked slowly along the beach in the moonlight, barefoot, and they'd skinny-dipped in velvet water.

And today they had spent their time lying in the sun, swimming, making love and talking about everything and anything except her father and what was going to happen tonight.

It was a time of getting to know each other again, finding out that although time had changed them so much, something hadn't changed at all.

Olivia slipped into a silk robe and looked at herself in the mirror. She barely recognized the woman who stared back. She was the same, but alive with an inner spark of energy—a passion that made her glow and made her eyes dance with light. It was as if she had finally been awakened after being somehow dead for the last decade and a half. Being with Jack had brought her back to life.

She cinched her robe tight, padded barefoot into the bedroom, sat on the white bed cover and reached for the phone. There was one more thing she had to do.

She called Grayson.

"My answer is no," she told him, before he could say anything else.

"Olivia?"

"I just wanted to let you know, Grayson, before—" *before midnight* "—before you heard it from someone else. I'm seeing another man. I have been for a while."

She couldn't bring herself to say she was sorry. She couldn't bring herself to say anything else. She thought of Lizzie's murder, of Grayson's deception, of his role in Jack's disappearance, of how he had wooed her, knowing all the while that he had murdered her cousin and destroyed her fiancé.

"Olivia, wait. Don't rush this—"

"It was you who wanted to rush, Grayson."

"Can you wait, just until—"

Her heart began to beat harder. *Until you become leader of the free world?*

"—next week, maybe."

"I wont feel any different next week, Grayson."

"You're with him now aren't you? You're with the arms dealer, Devilliers."

She felt a sick twist in her stomach. So her father *had* told him. Grayson knew she was seeing someone else, and he hadn't called her. He was playing her. They both were. Bitterness filled her mouth. "I'll get the ring back to you somehow."

"I don't want the ring, Olivia. I want you."

"Goodbye, Grayson." She hung up. She blew out a stream of breath, and a weight lifted from her shoulders. She'd just said farewell to sixteen fraudulent years.

It's what happens next that matters.

Jack's words wove through her mind. But she felt better equipped for what lay ahead now. She was committed to seeing Grayson Forbes in prison, and she was ready to confront her father.

She stepped barefoot onto sun-warmed terra-cotta tiles and into the soft golden haze of late-afternoon sunlight. She caught her breath at the sigh of Jack. His torso was darkly bronzed from the sun, and the color of his skin contrasted starkly against the bright white of the loose cotton drawstring pants slung low on his hips.

He turned round and smiled, his eyes as light as the sky behind him. He motioned to the drinks tray. "Can I fix you something cold? Gin and tonic?"

"That would be wonderful." She walked up to the balustrade and felt the soft breeze through her hair.

He came to her side, held out her drink. Ice chinked as she took it, their fingers brushing.

But he stilled, an unfathomable look filling his eyes. He removed the drink from her hand, set it on the balustrade and took both her hands in his.

Anxiety rippled through her. "What is it, Jack?"

"I wasn't going to say this, not until after, because I'm not sure where we'll all be after midnight."

Her pulse quickened.

"Sixteen years ago I wanted to spend the rest of my life with you." His eyes held hers. "I still do. I still want you to marry me, Olivia."

Her heart began to pound so hard she couldn't breathe, couldn't talk.

"I've thought about it," he said. "No matter where you want to live, I can make it work…on São Diogo Island, or in Manhattan, anywhere. We've been wanting to set up a U.S. office for some time now. And if—"

"Jack, I—"

"No!" He narrowed his eyes. "Don't say anything, not now. Not until—" he hesitated "—not until you've thought about it properly. But whatever happens tonight, know, Olivia, that *this* is what I want. I never want to lose you. Not again."

"Jack…you're scaring me."

His eyes burned. He grabbed her, kissed her, hard

and long and deep and desperate. And when he pulled away, she was breathless, her blood pounding, and she saw a raw anguish in his features.

"I love you more than anything, Livie," he whispered, his voice gravelly with emotion.

"Jack…you're not thinking of going and dying on me now, are you?"

His lip twitched. "Done that already—death is not what it's cracked up to be. No, now I'm thinking of how much living we still have to do, how much time we have to make up. We're still good together, Olivia. Don't you think?"

"Better than good, Jack. It's better than ever."

Relief sifted into his eyes, and Olivia was moved to see it. Her warrior was vulnerable. He cared so much about her that he was afraid. She could not have loved him more than at that moment.

She didn't need to think. Of course she was going to say yes. She couldn't imagine any other future, didn't want to, not without him.

He checked his watch and inhaled deeply. "It's time."

20:14 Romeo. Caribbean Sea.
Monday, October 13.

Olivia stood beside Jack on the small yacht as they chugged out of the harbor, leaving the twinkling lights that lined the bay. They headed into dark water.

But the moon was almost full, the milky way miraculous, and there was a soft, salty breeze that ruffled the ends of her red dress. She knew it looked good on her. She hadn't felt more glamorous in a long time. And

Jack looked simply spectacular, as if he'd stepped straight off the pages of a high-powered men's magazine. What his body did for a tux should be declared illegal.

She watched the churning white wake behind their boat, trying not to think of what lay ahead, of tomorrow.

"Why did you do that?" he asked her out of the darkness.

She glanced up at him and smiled, glad for the diversion. "You mean why did I just hand a diamond ring worth hundreds of thousands of dollars to that couple standing on the dock?"

He grinned. "Yeah, that would be what I mean."

Her smile deepened. "They looked so much in love, Jack. And they were as young as we were when you first proposed to me. Besides, I didn't want the ring any more. I didn't want any part of him near me. Ever again."

"He didn't want it back?"

She shook her head. "No. Maybe that couple can sell it, get a small start. Maybe they can have a chance, one we never got."

He touched her face. "You're beautiful, you know that? Inside, not just on the outside. It's why I first fell in love with you."

She looked into his eyes and realized with mild shock that they were pale gray—almost silver in the moonlight. "You're not wearing your contacts, Jack!"

"Henri has served his purpose, Olivia. Jack is back. Now I want your father to recognize me."

Panic nudged her. "You…want to shock him?"

He nodded. "I'll need the edge. I need to get straight to the point. We'll have less than an hour."

"If he sees it's you, if he sees that you're alive and with me, that you're not Henri, he'll know immediately that I am betraying him, that I've helped set him up."

He studied her quietly. Then he took something out of his pocket, held it in the palm of his hand. It glinted in the moonlight. She stared.

"You left this in your bathroom."

"My Saint Catherine pendant?"

He let it dangle through his fingers, the small disc spinning in the moonlight.

"You fixed it."

"Do you remember why I gave this to you, Livie?"

"Of course." She hesitated. "It's the reason I kept it, why I kept on wearing it."

"Saint Catherine of Alexandra," he said, "patron saint of lawyers, a learned lady who argued for what she believed in, who held true to her beliefs, stuck to her course."

She lifted her eyes to his, the innuendo dead clear.

"Will you wear it tonight, for me?"

Tension tightened her stomach. "Yes," she whispered. "Yes, I will." She turned around, lifted her hair up, bent her head forward. He looped the chain around her and fastened the clasp at the back of her neck.

She placed her fingers over the pendant, turned back to face him, wearing the symbol he'd given her in law school. It was a time when the world—their future— still lay at their feet, bright with promise. It was a time when they were both committed to righting wrongs, fighting for global justice—naive ideals maybe, but that's where dreams start, and from them a reality is fashioned. They never really had the opportunity to do that. It had been stolen from them.

"A second chance," he whispered, and kissed her lightly on the cheek.

Olivia turned to watch as they approached her father's yacht—a bank of glimmering layers of light. Snatches of music reached them on the breeze, then were drowned out as some of his guests arrived by helicopter. The tension in her stomach coiled tighter.

The trouble with Saint Catherine was that she'd died for her beliefs.

A week ago Olivia might have been ready to die for what she believed in. But now Jack was back. Now she had too much to live for.

"One hour to midnight," he said as their craft bumped up alongside the *Genevieve*.

Jack adjusted the small communications device in his ear as they knocked softly against the *Genevieve's* hull. "Can you hear me," he said quietly.

"Affirmative," McDonough responded.

Jack was now in contact with his teams. He reached for Olivia's hand, grasped it firmly. "Show-time," he murmured.

Security personnel waited up on deck. Underneath the vessel, Jack's divers circled like hungry sharks, and on the surface, out of obvious range, his men waited for his order to close in. They had the *Genevieve* surrounded.

He held his arms out, noting camera positions as the security guards patted him down. It was eight minutes after eleven. Arriving any sooner might have given Killinger too much time to come up with backup. Any later, and they might not stop the bombs.

The guards politely asked if they could remove the two guns and the knife they'd found. "But of course," he said in his best French-Belgian accent, and they waved him forward.

They hadn't found the detonator, or the syringe and vial in the compartment hidden in his shoe. He slid his hand proprietarily around Olivia's waist, and for a brief moment he allowed himself to enjoy the delicious slip of blood-red silk under his fingers.

He escorted her toward a covered area of the deck lined with hundreds of tiny white lights. A sumptuous buffet complete with ice carvings, Alaskan crab, lobster and caviar was set off to the left. The remainder of the area was filled with guests who exuded the distinct scent of wealth. Diamonds flashed, music tinkled, glasses chinked, and people laughed lightly.

He guided Olivia through the sophisticated crowd and toward the bar. Olivia nodded and smiled, greeting people she recognized. Jack felt absurdly proud to be at her side, to be here, as himself, as her lover.

He heard McDonough's voice in his ear telling him that it looked as if there was now only one man in the stateroom that served as Killinger's office. FDS divers had determined this using underwater infrared equipment beneath the boat.

It was time to make his move.

Killinger was most likely watching his guests through the cameras he had mounted everywhere. Jack looked up and stared directly into one.

Killinger was hugely relieved to learn his daughter's boat had finally arrived. Olivia was safely on his turf. He was back in control.

He'd instructed his guards to bring Devilliers to see him right after Elliot's televised press conference. He wanted to meet this man before he had him eliminated. A part of him was intrigued. He wanted to see for himself what attracted his daughter to the notorious Belgian arms dealer.

Killinger checked his watch—forty-nine minutes and it would all be over. Maybe he needn't worry about the fact that his assassin had not shown up yet. So far everything was still going to go according to plan. He could deal with his assassin after the trasfer of power.

He glanced at the bank of plasma screens that lined one wall of his office. The smaller screens were part of his onboard security surveillance system, the bigger screens he'd had installed to monitor the top news channels, as the world and its reporters readied themselves for the president's press conference. He'd had one of his White House insiders leak the news of the president's failing health to a CBNN correspondent, just to put Elliot on edge, to remind him that the Cabal was here, waiting, and to make the world sit up and notice.

Forty-five minutes to go now. He turned his attention to the bank of security screens and watched his guests. Something instantly caught his attention. A man captured by camera nine looked right at him, right into his stateroom, a direct challenge in his eyes. Killinger went stone still.

His heart began to race. *Devilliers?* He hit a button, froze the frame, zoomed in.

That haunting feeling surfaced again as he looked into the man's eyes. They were ice gray—like a dangerous wolf.

Killinger's blood turned cold. He *knew* where he'd seen those eyes before. Perspiration prickled over his lip. His heart began to race. He zoomed in closer. The man's angular face and violent scar filled his vision, his room, his very soul.

By God.

He felt faint. Could it be? Could it really be him?

Jack Sauer?

Alive?

His daughter knew. If this was not Henri, if this was Jack, back from the dead or God knows where, then Olivia must know that her fiancé was not the one who had killed Elizabeth. Did she know what he was doing *now?*

His head was spinning.

What in hell did Jack have to do with any of *this?* Where had he been all this time? And that elaborate cover of Henri Devilliers, everything had checked out…. Killinger cursed violently.

He'd been duped.

He turned back to the bank of screens, panic and confusion licking through his body. On one of the television channels an anchor was announcing that the president was getting ready to address the nation. Killinger's guard knocked, opened the door to his stateroom. Killinger spun round, nerves biting at him.

"Thirty-eight minutes to go, sir. Would you like me to link the feeds through to the ballroom?"

"No! No, not yet."

Damn, he was not in control here. His eyes shot back to the bank of security cameras, and his heart clean stopped.

The assassin was boarding the yacht. His security guards were patting him down, surrounding him. Killinger had told his men that the man would be using the name Frobisher, and that under the pretext of escorting him to his office, they were to take him down into the hold, detain him until he could be interrogated. And then killed.

Killinger's eyes followed from camera to camera as his guards led the albino past the buffet table. But the assassin stopped suddenly, right in front of Olivia.

Every nerve in Killinger's body coiled tight. He zoomed in quickly, the man's words snaking through his brain....

She looks like your wife.

The bastard was trying to rattle him. Then Killinger caught sight of Jack. He was staring at the albino, his wolf eyes narrow and dangerous. Killinger zoomed even closer, his hands trembling. Jack's body was strung like wire as he stared at the albino.

He knew him!

Killinger could barely breathe. How would Jack Sauer know this man? He hit the communications button. "Bring Frobisher to me. I must speak with him. *At once!*"

* * *

Jack looked into the strange pale eyes of the man in front of him. He was well over six feet tall, built like a ship. This was without question the man who had killed December and escaped from São Diogo.

Violence coursed through him. What in hell was he doing here, on the yacht, now? This man knew about the FDS, about Dr. Sterling…why hadn't he told Killinger? Why hadn't the bombs gone off?

Unless he hadn't told him. *Yet.*

He had to stop him. Jack had to get to Killinger before this man did.

He bent down, whispered in Olivia's ear. "I need your help." He gestured to the albino. "Do *whatever* you can to distract him. Charm him, talk to him, make a scene, anything. I *must* get to your father before he does."

"Why?" she whispered

"He killed my man. He knows about the FDS."

"What does he want?"

"I have no idea what his game is. I think he's a loose cannon. Go. Now. Just make sure you have your father's guards around you at all times—they won't let him hurt you, I guarantee it."

Jack opened the door to Samuel Killinger's stateroom, entered as silently as a ghost and locked the door behind him. He'd left the guard lying unconscious outside.

Killinger was standing with his back to him, fixated with the image of his daughter talking to the albino, totally oblivious to his entry.

"Samuel."

Killinger turned slowly to face him. Jack's heart accelerated slightly. Killinger had been expecting him.

The first thought that hit Jack's mind as he looked into the face of his nemesis was that the man had aged. And strangely enough, the rage that had fueled him up until now suddenly dissipated. He felt incredibly calm, as if he were in some other medium, moving slowly through warped time, playing out a scene he'd been destined to play from his birth.

"Jack Sauer," Killinger said, studying him. "You're alive." His voice was still strong. It still held a deceiving and deadly warmth. Even with age, the man was just as powerful in person as Jack remembered. Yet there was an air of vulnerability about him. Maybe it had always been there. Maybe he could just see it now because he, too, was older and hopefully wiser.

Or maybe he just understood how a woman like Olivia could make a man vulnerable

"I made a mistake, Jack."

"You made many mistakes, Samuel." Jack said moving closer, using the man's first name.

Killinger stiffened, squaring his shoulders. "No," he said slowly. "I made only one. I underestimated you. What do you want, Jack? Why have you come back?" He began to edge toward the console as he spoke, his hand fingering along the counter toward the control buttons.

"I wouldn't touch those controls, Samuel, not if you value your daughter's life."

Killingers eyes flickered sharply. "What do you mean?" he spoke cautiously, calmly, but Jack knew his brain had to be racing a million miles a minute, searching for escape routes. "Is it revenge you're looking for?"

Behind him, above the screens showing repeated images of Elliot and Ruger, a digital clock read twenty-nine minutes. It flipped to twenty-eight. It was counting down.

"Justice, not revenge. And I will get it. But that's not why I'm back. I want you to call off the biological attack."

Killinger paled.

The clock clicked down to twenty-seven minutes.

"How do you know about the bombs? What does any of this have to do with you?"

"I'm here on behalf of the president."

Killinger's body twitched, but his features remained unchanged.

Jack extracted the chain from under the collar of his dress shirt and yanked the detonator tab free. He flicked the tab open, positioned his thumb over the pad, held it up for Killinger to see.

A news anchor on one of the channels announced that the president was preparing to take the podium. Another channel showed Elliot and Ruger talking intimately, seriously. Yet another channel focused on Grayson Forbes waiting in the wings, his face grave.

The clock flipped to twenty-six minutes.

"Call off that conference, Samuel. And call off the attack or I press this button and your daughter dies."

His eyes flickered sharply but he remained silent.

Jack stepped closer. "Why don't you turn around, take a look at that screen behind you. See the silver bracelet on her arm?"

Killinger held Jack's eyes for a moment, then he turned, very slowly, and stared at the screen. "I see it," he said. "Olivia told me that bracelet was given to her by a friend…." His voice faded as he put two and two together.

"If I press this button, that bracelet will inject a pathogen into her arm—a prion disease designed in *your* Nexus lab."

He whirled round, eyes wide.

"Oh, it's not the same one you plan to release over New York, Los Angles and Chicago, Samuel. You do not have the antidote for this one."

He stared at Jack, breathing hard, desperation filling his eyes.

The clock clicked down to twenty-five minutes. Silence stretched.

"Call it off, Samuel."

"I *can't*. The protocols are already in place. The pathogen will be released at five after midnight. There's nothing I can do to stop it."

Jack raised the detonator. "Then Olivia dies, at your hand, with your pathogen. Ironic, isn't it, Samuel?"

"I want her in here!" he demanded. "I need to see her. Now!"

Jack knew what he was doing. Killinger was aware of how much Jack had once loved his daughter, and he was going to gamble with that. He was betting that Jack could not look into Olivia's eyes and still press that button.

"Fine," Jack said slowly, his eyes on the clock. "Have her brought in. But one wrong move and I promise you she *will* die. Don't think I haven't got it in me."

Killinger's eyes narrowed and his lips curled. "So *this* is your idea of revenge, is it, Jack?" he hissed. "To take her away from me, the one thing I truly care about? To destroy my life—"

"Like you destroyed mine?"

"Hurting Olivia will solve nothing, Jack! Leave her out of this, dammit!"

Jack watched the clock tick down another minute. "You have less than fifteen minutes to make up your mind, Samuel. Does she live—or die?"

Killinger glared at him. Tension pulsed in his neck. The clock ticked down to fourteen minutes. Then thirteen. Jack didn't blink.

Killinger spun round suddenly, depressed a button on the console. "Bring my daughter to me. At once."

The men faced each other, waiting for the woman they both loved to arrive. The clock ticked to twelve minutes.

On the monitors behind Killinger, Jack could see Elliot moving toward the microphones. All the news channels now had variations of the same shot. His mouth went dry. Tension squeezed his throat. But still he didn't blink. In eleven minutes the world could change.

Unless he stopped it.

The door flew open. Olivia burst through it, then froze. "Dad! Jack?"

Jack spoke first, his heart thudding. "Come here, Olivia."

She hesitated, her eyes fixed on her father, her face a storm of emotions. "What's going on?" she whispered.

"Just come here now." She moved to his side as he kept his eyes trained on her father. "You now have less than ten minutes to save your daughter's life, Samuel. Stop those bombs, or I press the button and detonate that cuff on your daughter's wrist. Then you can watch her die."

"Jack!" Olivia gasped.

His chest clenched. He tried to swallow, refusing to look at her. He *couldn't* look at her. He wouldn't be able to press the button if he did.

The clock ticked—*eight minutes*.

"She'll start to bleed internally almost immediately. Without an antidote, death will come in less than twelve hours."

A strange noise escaped Olivia's throat.

Something hot flashed in Killinger's face and his fist balled. "I told you, I *can't* stop this! The bombs are programmed to go. There's *nothing* I can do now."

Six minutes.

In all the television screens, Elliot was now at the podium, in front of a bank of microphones. Cameras zoomed in on his face.

A bead of perspiration trickled slowly down Jack's temple. Killinger didn't move. Silence pulsed heavily.

Four minutes.

"Dad…" Olivia pleaded in a hoarse whisper. "Please, Dad, for God's sake, don't let him do this! Please, Dad, stop the attack! Stop this thing. *Please!*"

Killinger's mouth flattened, his eyes hardened. No one moved.

Three minutes.

Two minutes.

The clock now began to count down the seconds—
1:59, 1:58, 1:57…

Jack turned, looked into Olivia's eyes and for a nanosecond, he almost faltered. *"Trust me,"* he whispered.

And he hit the button.

Chapter 14

23:59 Romeo. Caribbean Sea.
Monday, October 13.

Olivia gasped as the needle exploded into her wrist. She stared in shock as a small dark trickle of blood dribbled down her hand.

And then all hell broke loose. The FDS team burst through the door and surrounded Killinger. The choppers could be heard approaching, buzzing low over the ship. There were gunshots up on deck, women screaming. Then there was the strange and sudden hush of the *Genevieve's* engines being cut.

On the bank of plasma screens, the president was speaking into the microphones. "On this day it gives me great…"

And in Jack's ear, he could hear McDonough's voice.

"The medics have landed, they're on their way down to the stateroom." Jack crouched down, popped the hidden compartment in his shoe and released the syringe. "Tell them to wait outside, McDonough," he said as cracked the vial and filled the syringe, "until I give word." He tested the syringe with a squirt of serum and then stood, one eye on the television monitors, his torso damp with perspiration, his heart pounding.

Blood was already trickling from Olivia's nose. Killinger fought Jack's men, trying desperately to get to his daughter as they restrained him.

Jack held up the syringe. "The antidote," he said loudly.

Killinger stilled.

All went quiet in the room.

"If she gets this within half an hour, she will make a full recovery. If not, she *will* die. This, Samuel, is your last chance."

Olivia choked, put her hand to her mouth. It came away dark with blood. Terror filled her eyes. "You lied to me, Jack," she whispered hoarsely. "I…*trusted* you…" She coughed again.

Jack could feel the muscle in his jaw pulsing. The president's words filled the room. "I am here tonight because…" Elliot was stalling, thought Jack, hoping the FDS would still come through. This was it. Now or never. The future of the nation, the world hung on this moment. The seconds ticked down to twenty-two, twenty-one, twenty…

He waited for one more beat, then spun on his heels and made for the door, his heart thumping so hard he could barely breathe, barely hear, his body drenched with sweat.

"Wait!"

Jack stilled, turned slowly.

Killinger looked suddenly smaller, crumpled, defeated. Old. "I'll do it." He picked up the phone, punched in a code and hit a number. Then he hit a quick-dial button. "Call off the speech, at once. Yes…I am sure. Now!" He replaced the receiver, inhaled deeply, turned to face Jack. "Save my daughter's life, give her the antidote."

But Jack waited, his eyes fixed on the screens, every muscle in his body strung wire tense. The clock ticked past midnight.

The screens showed a White House aide moving up to the podium, whispering in the president's ear. John Elliot's body slumped with momentary relief. He closed his eyes for a second, his tension evident in the way his hands gripped the sides of the podium. Then he looked up, right into the cameras, right into Killinger's stateroom, the image repeated over and over and over in the bank of screens. He smiled—a tired smile, but still a smile.

Jack's heart swooped.

"Fellow citizens, tonight is a night that will go down in history. Tonight, because of a few brave men, I am able to stand before you and tell you that this country has avoided a terrorist attack of catastrophic proportions, an attack that…"

Emotion exploded into Jack's eyes. He spun round, dropped to his knees, took Olivia's arm. Her eyes were closed, her skin deathly pale and cold. He quickly tapped her vein and injected the antidote into her arm. "Get the medics in here, now!" he yelled as he fed the serum carefully into her system.

The door crashed open. The medics made for Olivia with a stretcher. Jack stroked her hand. "Olivia, you're going to be fine. *Trust me*."

She refused to open her eyes. "Leave me alone, please," she whispered faintly. "I never want to see you again."

"Livie—"

She turned her face away from him, and the medics took her…and they took Jack's heart with them.

Jack gritted his teeth, clenched his fists and closed his eyes tight. "Get that bastard the hell out of my sight," he growled, without looking at Killinger. "Notify the authorities. Hand him over."

He pinched the bridge of nose as his men took Samuel Killinger.

He'd saved a nation. But he'd lost the woman he loved. For the second time.

Jack made his way woodenly up to the top deck, stepped into the sea air and dragged both hands over his hair. He watched the spinning blades of the helicopter as they gathered speed, ready to evacuate Olivia to the nearest hospital.

In the back of his mind he heard a gunshot below deck. He paid no attention. He knew his men were in control. His job was done. It was over—in more ways than one.

He watched the chopper rise. And he wondered if it had been worth it.

McDonough came up behind him. "Sauvage, we have a problem."

Jack registered the use of his French name in some distant part of his brain. "What is it?" he said, watching the pulsing lights of the chopper grow smaller and smaller in the night sky.

"It's the albino—he took Killinger out. He was in the hold…he went for Killinger before anyone realized what was happening. He had a knife."

"Killinger's dead?" Jack felt nothing, just hollow.

"Yes."

"The albino?"

"Our men shot him. They're both gone. I'm sorry."

"It's better that way," he said as the lights of the helicopter were swallowed completely by the darkness of the Caribbean night.

McDonough watched them disappear, too. "We did it, Sauvage," he said quietly. "A mission impossible. We saved the bloody nation."

"We didn't save the president. He's going to die."

"You did your job, Jacques. We did our best—"

"It's Jack."

McDonough hesitated. "Sorry, mate. Force of habit."

Jack nodded, his eyes fixed on the black sky where Olivia's chopper had disappeared from sight.

McDonough hit him on the shoulder. "No one ever said sacrifice was easy, *mon ami*."

12:05 Romeo Manhattan.
Wednesday, December 24.

Olivia stood at her window, watching snow fall softly over New York—big fat fairy-tale flakes, drifting slowly, swirling, settling fast on the cold streets, blanketing the city for Christmas Eve. The television was on in the background and President Michael J. Taylor was giving a speech.

A deep sadness filled her heart. It would be the first Christmas that she would spend truly alone. No family at all.

She hugged her arms over her stomach. She'd lost a lot of weight. She was still tired. She'd attended her father's funeral, and she'd attended President Elliot's funeral—one man buried a hero, the other a villain. Her eyes burned at the thought of her father. But no more tears would come.

Grayson was being detained, his trial pending, the media going berserk over it all. She herself had been subjected to weeks of interrogation by countless agencies and bureaucracies. And through it all, Jack had been…nowhere.

He'd used her in the most devastating way. Even his marriage proposal had been a tool to buy her absolute faith in him so that she would betray her father.

Now they were both gone—Jack and her dad.

She had no one.

She needed to find the strength to stand on her own again. Totally on her own. She had to think about going back to work again. She'd taken enough time off.

She glanced at the television, the emotion in Taylor's voice suddenly snaring her attention. She moved closer to the television set, turned it up, watched. He was rallying the nation in the wake of the death of a beloved man. He was talking about overcoming the cancers of the past, about meeting challenges head-on, about healing and forgiving, about the work ahead in the New Year.

Olivia turned again to look at the snow. It was getting thick now, and the world looked clean. She smiled sadly. Mother Nature was doing her bit, cleaning up the world, making it beautiful before it segued into a New Year. A new time. A new era for this country.

She inhaled deeply. Jack had done his bit to get them this far.

What would you do, Olivia? One life to save millions?

His words echoed through her mind, words spoken in this very apartment. She reached up, felt for the Saint Catherine's pendant around her neck. She held it, thinking about the dreams, the goals, the ideals they had once shared, so many years ago.

They were all still there at the root of it all, she thought—all those same beliefs. If she had been Jack, if she had been faced with this mission, this conflict, she wouldn't have had a choice, either.

She could see that now, with hindsight, that Jack had consistently been true to himself, to his morals. If anyone had been constant at all, in all these years, it had been Jack.

She should be proud of what he did. And she was. It just hurt so bad. She knew she'd said she never wanted to see him again—but it still hurt that he hadn't come back, that he hadn't been there to support her through all the stuff she'd had to go through.

She fingered the pendant. What should she expect?

But Taylor was right. It was time to forgive, to move on, to look ahead to the new challenges, even if she had to do that alone now. She was a fighter, and she wasn't going to go down. Not after what she'd been through.

Her cell phone chimed. She reached for it, answered, watching the mesmerizing swirl of flakes.

It was Harvey. He wanted her to come in to the office to join them all for an early Christmas Eve gathering before everyone headed home.

"Starts at three-thirty," he said.

"Harvey, I don't think so. I…I'm not in the mood."

"We have eggnog."

"Yeah? Now I'm *really* not coming."

He laughed, then his voice turned serious. "Olivia, you need to get out. Who else are you going to spend Christmas Eve with?"

"I…I have friends."

"Yeah? And we're all here, waiting for you."

She glanced at Taylor's image on the screen.

Time to move on.

"Okay," she said. "I'll come."

Harvey hung up and grinned broadly. "She's coming."

Jack grasped his shoulder. "Thank you, mate, I owe you."

"Hey, I'm doing this for her, not you."

Jack nodded. "Still, I owe you, and I never forget a favor."

Olivia saw him standing in the early dusk under the United Nations flag of peace, snow over his big black coat, a tangle of wilting pink and white flowers in his gloved hands.

She froze in her tracks. Part of her almost turned and ran. From what, she wasn't sure—fear that he'd come to say goodbye, farewell?

She swallowed, braced, walked slowly toward him, the snow soft under her boots.

"So Harvey set me up?" she said as she neared him.

"Olivia," he whispered. "Damn, it's good to see you."

"Where have you been, Jack?"

"Tying up loose ends with Elliot before he died. Debriefings. Getting to know President Taylor, bringing him up to speed with what happened. Dealing with the CIA, the Feds. Everyone's trying to clean house. It'll take some time."

She nodded. "I see."

Jack hesitated. "I also wanted to give *you* time, Olivia."

"For what?"

"To hate me. To grieve. To think. Assimilate. I didn't want to pressure you. You needed to work this out without me around. I think if I had stayed, you might have hated me forever. I don't want you to hate me, Olivia."

She swallowed against the tight pain in her throat. "Your FDS profiler might know an awful lot about psychology, but *you* sure as hell know nothing, Jack."

He raised his hand to touch her, but she backed away, afraid of connecting with him. Afraid that if she did, she'd lose herself in him, get hurt all over again.

"I'm sorry, Olivia. I…I'm doing the best I know how."

She stared at him, the flowers, the vulnerability in his eyes.

"Why did you get Harvey to call, Jack?" she asked quietly.

"I was afraid you might not speak to me."

"You're leaving, aren't you?"

He nodded. "Tonight."

She looked down at her feet. "Was *anything* about us true?"

"*Everything* was true, Olivia. Not once has there been anything false about my feelings for you."

She scuffed her boot in the snow. "You lied to me, Jack. You could have trusted me. I believed in you. I picked my side. I found the courage within myself to defy my father, and I would *not* have let you down." She looked up, met his eyes. "But *you* just couldn't find it within yourself to trust me, could you?"

She turned, took two steps away, her heart racing, then she whirled back to face him. "I could have pulled that charade off. But you thought I was too weak. You just *had* to inject a live pathogen into my system."

He closed his eyes for a moment. "I did trust you, Olivia. But the cuff was still necessary. Your fear had to be real. Samuel Killinger was not a man you could bluff easily. If your fear had not been real, if that pathogen had not been real, he would not have stopped those bombs. *We* would not be standing here." His eyes pierced hers. "I never intended to hurt you, Olivia, ever. I would never have let it go too far."

She looked at the delicate long-stemmed and frothy flowers hanging limp over his powerful arms. "What do you want, Jack?"

"I want you to find it in your heart to forgive me, Olivia. Can you try to understand what I was dealing with?"

She looked down at her feet again, and she kicked the tip of her boot gently into the deepening snow, conscious of the strange hush over the city, the surreal purple-white light. "Maybe you need to forgive yourself, Jack. Maybe some things cannot be understood."

"A wise man told you that once, right?"

She glanced up, almost smiled. "Yes. A wise man who drove a white Lamborghini. He also said, 'It's what happens next that matters.'"

"This wise man have a French accent?"

This time she did smile. "Yeah, he did."

"Did he also just happen to mention that you don't get a third chance?"

"Not…exactly."

"Livie, we *won't* get a third chance. We have to get it right this time." He paused. "Do you remember what I said? I told you that no matter what happened, I never wanted to lose you again. I meant it. I still mean it."

She paused. "Why did you come here, Jack? To say goodbye? Because—"

He held out the armful of sad flowers. "Do you have *any* idea how hard it was to get these?"

She frowned in confusion. "No, I don't, but they sure don't look happy."

"They're cosmos, Olivia. They grow in my garden, and they bloom all summer long."

"You have a garden?"

He grinned sheepishly, his mouth so sexily crooked. "I do now. I bought a house earlier this month. And yes, it has a garden." His eyes brightened as he spoke. "It overlooks the Atlantic—you can walk right down onto the beach, and you can watch the sunset from the porch. It's summer there now, and the cosmos are blooming all along the bottom fence."

She thought she had no tears left, but they filled her eyes anyway.

He pushed the flowers into her hands. "They're for you, Livie. I wanted you to get a small taste of what it might be like."

She touched the fragile blooms. "Might be like?"

"When you get there, to São Diogo." He hesitated, the vulnerability back in his features. "I have *two* seats booked on that plane tonight."

"Jack—"

He held up his hands. "And just in case you haven't been watching the news, I'm a free man in my own land now—you don't have to be embarrassed to be seen on Jack Sauer's arm. You can be proud, Olivia, to be with me now."

Tears flooded her eyes. "What…what *is* this, Jack?"

His eyes turned serious. "It's a proposal, Livie. I want you to come back with me. I want you to marry me. This is the last shot we're going to get to make this work."

Emotion sliced through her, and she blinked sharply. "My…apartment…my job—"

"You can come back if you don't like it there. Or I can come back with you if you want to live in Manhattan. There's no pressure, Livie. No strings, carte blanche. All I want is to not have to leave without you tonight." He angled his head. "And to spend Christmas with you. More than anything I want to spend Christmas with you."

Emotion choked her throat, stole her voice.

"I love you, Olivia. I always have, and I always will, whether you come with me tonight or not, but please… tell me you will come."

She looked into those incredible eyes. She loved him, too, always had and always would—even though he'd hurt her. And Lord knew she'd hurt him, too.

A time to forgive—that's what President Taylor had said. A time to heal the past. Would she ever forgive herself if she walked away from him now? *Could* she even walk away?

This man was her destiny.

"We could get re-engaged," he offered. "You could take your time to get to know me better."

She touched the wilting petals and smiled. "I don't recall actually breaking the engagement off, Jack. And I don't believe there's a statute of limitations on these things."

"Does that mean you'll be on that plane with me?"

She closed her eyes. What did she have in New York? Nothing, if she really thought about it. The future was wide open—the way it had been the day they were first engaged. She opened her eyes, bit her lip. "Yes, Jack."

He sucked in his breath sharply.

"I will be on that plane with you." She touched the flowers again, and her heart squeezed. "I want to see your garden," she whispered. "We can take it one day at a time," she said softly, and lifted her eyes. "Can't we?"

Tears glistened in her mercenary's eyes.

He nodded. "I've waited a long time for you, Livie."

He stepped close to her, brushed snow from her hair, hooked his gloved knuckle under her chin. "But every minute of those years has been worth it…for this."

And he kissed the woman he'd never stopped loving in the swirling flakes, the world hushed by snow, just the soft flap of the United Nations flag of peace up over their heads.

And Jack knew, finally, he was home.

Epilogue

Three years later. Camp David.

Jack put his napkin on the table and leaned back in his chair. The sun was warm, and the lunch had been excellent. He reached over, squeezed his wife's hand. She smiled at him. Olivia looked so relaxed, so happy. Pregnancy had done beautiful things to her body and her face, and the light of life showed in her honey-gold eyes.

He was here with Sarah and Hunter McBride, who were watching their daughter, Branna, run over the grass, her little brown legs chubby, her feet bare, the sun shining on her dark hair. The little girl was a precious example of what could come from tragedy, thought Jack. She was already shaping up to break a thousand hearts.

Also at Camp David on this afternoon, at the invitation of President Taylor and the first lady, was Sultan Rafiq bin Zafir bin Omar al-Qaadr and his beautiful queen, Dr. Paige Sterling.

Without these people, sitting around this table under a warm summer sun, their mission three years ago would not have been a success.

And without the love that they had all discovered amid danger, the future would not have been possible.

Jack raised his glass. I'd like to propose a toast," he said. "To Dr. McBride," he looked at Hunter. "Congratulations, my friend."

Hunter had recently requalified and was now working as FDS chief surgeon at the São Diogo hospital.

Jack turned to Rafiq. "And to the Sultan—" he raised his glass "—to peace in Hamān."

Rafiq grinned, raised his glass. He and the president had spent the morning talking Middle-East policy, and they were pleased with the results.

The president lifted his glass, joining the toast. "To my men." He'd called them that for the past three years. It was a fond reference to what had passed between them, to what they had done for his country.

"And to their three very special ladies. Without you all—" his eyes turned serious "—the world would be a very different place."

"And to President Elliot," said Jack raising his glass higher. "A great man."

"Cheers," they said in quiet unison. And they drank silently, thinking about the heroes they had lost along the way.

And about what they had won.

Jack reached for Olivia's hand under the table. He knew she was thinking of her father, about the relationship of parent and child.

"He'd be happy for you," he whispered.

She smiled gently. "I know, Jack." She paused. "It's better this way." She looked into his eyes. "You'll make a great father, you know."

He winked. "*And* I can cook."

She laughed, and his world was complete.

* * * *

For an exclusive extract from next month's
Juliet's Law *by Ruth Wind, turn the page!*

"Ready?" her sister asked, putting sunglasses on her head.

"I am."

A woman in a yellow jacket moved by the table and gave Desi a long, hard glare. Desi stared right back. When the woman continued toward the cash register, Desi and rolled her eyes at Juliet. "The dentist's wife," she said when the woman had gone outside. "She hates my guts."

"Because?"

"Because she's one of Claude's groupies, and in their eyes, I'm just a mean woman who doesn't understand him."

"Yeah," Josh said, behind them, "you old meanie, you."

Desi grinned, her eyes flashing in a way that made her sister wonder what had forged the bond between these two.

And was there something romantic brewing? "You better believe it, mister."

Did her sister have feelings for this man? He was sort of her type, after all, a rugged Native American, an outdoorsman. He had that adorable daughter who needed a mother.

Josh laughed softly, and Juliet felt the sound run down her neck like warm fingers. She resisted looking up at him, getting caught again in that dark, patient gaze. But even as she resisted, she felt the steady presence of him at her back, solid, steady, calm, and she couldn't help the wave of yearning it kindled in her. It had been a long time since Juliet had felt safe—if she ever had.

Scott was a good man—smart, supportive, ambitious—but she'd never felt sheltered by him. Josh, on the other hand—

With a popping little shock, she heard her thoughts. *Stop it!* She was engaged! It was one thing to admire the long, sturdy thighs of a man, or the grace of his hands. A woman had eyes, after all….

But it was something else again to be thinking of resting against that broad shoulder, to imagine taking a deep breath of relief as that deep laughter rang into the room.

Disloyal. In two directions if Desi was attracted to him, too.

Blindly, Juliet stood and walked towards the door, grabbing a green-and-brown-wrapped mint from a bowl on the counter. "I'll be right outside," she called back. Without waiting for a reply, she rushed out.

The door was in a little foyer with racks of newspapers and tourist brochures on one side. As Juliet rushed through, a man was coming in, and Juliet stepped aside, and—

Slammed squarely into her demons. She was never quite sure what happened, why she was flung back in time, but suddenly, she smelled a musky aftershave and margaritas, and there was a swooshing of all sound, as if her ears were covered. In real time, she ducked her head and managed to stumble around the man coming in the door, ignoring him when he said, "Miss, are you all right?" and got out to the sunshine in the street. Sweat poured down the back of her neck.

But even in the bright sunshine and open air, her throat felt constricted, and her breath came in ragged, tearing gasps. The worst was the sense of mindless panic urging her to *flee! flee! flee!* Her legs burned with the need, her lungs felt as if they would explode. With as much control as she could muster, she grabbed the stone corner of the building and leaned on it, trying not to fight the sensations nor give into them.

A heavy hand fell on her shoulder. "Hey, Juliet, are you—"

She screamed, slammed the hand away. Tried to back off, bumped into the wall.

Saw that it was Josh, and wanted to burst into tears.

He held his hands up, palm out to show he wouldn't hurt her. "Hey, hey, hey," he said. That rich gentle voice splashed into her panic, coating it like chocolate.

And just as suddenly as she'd been sucked into the flashback, she fell back out. With a soft noise, Juliet pitched forward, instinctively reaching for the sturdiness of his big, strong shoulders. Her head landed against his sternum, and she could smell the clean freshness of clothes hung out to dry on a line, and something deeper, his flesh. A gentle light hand smoothed her hair.

"You're okay," he said. "You're okay."

And it was true. After a moment, the dark memories retreated, and she could take a long, slow breath. Raise her head. Only then did she realize how close they were. Embarrassed, she tried to take a step back, and bumped into the wall at her back. "I'm sorry," she said, trying to duck to her left, afraid to look at him.

"Easy." He moved his big hand up and down her arm. "You don't have to go anywhere. Your sister will be here in a hot second."

"I'm—this is…oh, I'm embarrassed." She bent her head. "Thanks. I'm sorry."

"You don't have to apologize." His rumbling voice again rolled down her spine, easing the tension there, and his hands kept moving on her arms in a most soothing way. Steady. Gentle. "You don't have to say anything at all."

Juliet bent her head. He wore dark brown leather hiking boots, sturdy-looking with laces and hooks and eyes and a sole that looked as if it could withstand six inches of ice. Her feet in their thin California boots looked insubstantial, tiny even, and with a glimmer of pleasure, she thought one of the reasons to like a man so big was so that you could feel small next to him. And she was not normally a small woman.

She wanted to offer an explanation, to say something to excuse her weird behavior. The flashbacks were hateful, like a scar, and it made her feel overwhelmed to imagine telling him. Where to start? "Thanks," was all she said.

He released her and in the next instant, Desi came out, offering breath mints to everyone. Juliet moved away, vaguely aware of him watching her. "We'd better get to the courthouse," she said. "Get this taken care of."

"Yep. Let's do it. "

Juliet glanced up at Josh. "See you later."

His eyes were steady and sober and saw far more than she wished. "Right."

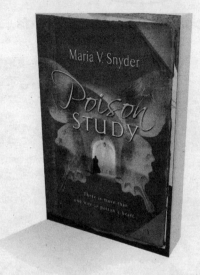

HURRICANE-SAVAGED NEW ORLEANS HAS A NEW DARK FORCE TO FEAR...

For police captain Patti O'Shea, the discovery of a dead body is shocking, but part of the job.

A dead body with the right hand severed is disturbing.

But when a corpse is discovered with the police badge of her murdered husband, she is pushed over the edge.

Driven by revenge, and working outside the law, Patti vows to track the monster responsible. But as the killings continue, it becomes clear that she is not the hunter – but the hunted.

Available 17th August 2007

FIRST CAME THE COVER-UP... THEN CAME THE NIGHTMARE

Florida

Investigating the disappearance of her boss, scientist Sabrina Gallows discovers a deadly secret that her employers will kill to keep hidden.

Washington, DC

Congressional aide Jason Brill suspects his boss's friendship with big business may be more of a liability than an asset.

Together, Sabrina and Jason are drawn into a sinister plot that puts corporate greed and corruption above human life. Each must race against time to reveal the truth about this unspeakable evil...

Available 19th October 2007

MIRA